Winding Valley Farm: Annie's Story

BY ANNE PELLOWSKI

pictures by WENDY WATSON

PHILOMEL BOOKS
New York

Also by Anne Pellowski

Willow Wind Farm: Betsy's Story
Stairstep Farm: Anna Rose's Story
The Nine Crying Dolls, a Story from Poland

First published in 1982 by Philomel Books,
a division of The Putnam Publishing Group,
200 Madison Avenue,
New York, N.Y. 10016.
Published simultaneously in Canada by
General Publishing Co. Limited, Toronto.
Text © 1982 by Anne Pellowski
Illustrations © 1982 by Wendy Watson
All rights reserved.
Printed in the United States of America.

Design and typography by Antler & Baldwin.

Library of Congress Cataloging in Publication Data
Pellowski, Anne.
Winding Valley farm.
Summary: A young girl shares pleasures and
disappointments with the other members of a large
Wisconsin farm family in the early twentieth century.
[1. Polish Americans—Fiction 2. Farm life—
Fiction. 3. Wisconsin—Fiction] I. Watson,
Wendy, ill. II. Title.
PZ7.P365Wi   [Fic]   81-15908
ISBN 0-399-20863-1   AACR2

Dedicated to the memory of
my mother and my father

I wish to thank the following relatives, classmates and friends of my parents for their help on many details, and for their general reminiscences:

Emeline Kulas Datta
Victor Pellowski
Eleanor Kaldunski Kratch
Emil Glenzinski
Eligia Maliszewski Glenzinski
The Losinski Family
Stella Gostkowski Pellowski
Robert Hoesley
Mary Wicka Bambenek
Felix Moga
Rev. Edward Stanek

Contents

The Seeds Get Blessed

On the morning of April 25, 1908, in the kitchen of a farmhouse in Wisconsin, a little girl was watching her mother sort out seed packets. Her name was really Anna Pelagia, but because her mother was also an Anna, she was called Annie.

Over in another corner of the kitchen, Annie's older sister, Sally, was helping the three youngest boys get washed and dressed. Roman was five years old, Leo was four and August was two, but they looked so much alike, with their red curly hair, that sometimes Annie had to look twice before she was sure which was which. They were giving Sally lots of trouble that morning because they did not want to get washed behind the ears.

"Behave yourselves, boys," said Annie's mother in Polish. Sometimes she spoke in Polish and sometimes in English. Usually when she was scolding them she did it in Polish.

"Should I put on their flannel shirts, Mother, or the cotton ones?" asked Sally. The children always called their parents "Mother" and "Father" when they answered in Polish, but in English they called them "Ma" and "Pa."

"I guess you can use the cotton ones. The weather has turned so nice it's more like summer than spring."

The door burst open and Annie's two older brothers came in from doing their chores. Joe was fourteen, the oldest, and John was eight and a half, exactly two years older than Annie. Sometimes she wished John were a girl; then maybe they wouldn't argue so much.

"Wash up quickly, boys, and get dressed for church."

"Oh, Ma, do we have to?" complained Joe. "Can't we stay here and do some planting or something? It's not a Sunday."

"Not go to church on spring Rogation Day?" Ma's voice sounded shocked. "Whatever are you thinking of? You should know we would not do any planting without getting the seeds blessed."

Annie could see Ma gently shaking her head at Joe and John.

"Won't the seeds grow if they aren't blessed?" she asked.

"Of course they'll grow," answered Ma. "But we don't want anything to happen while they are growing. A blessing asks God to protect them. And we have to thank the good Lord that we have seeds to plant at all."

They heard the sound of feet scraping on the step outside the door.

"Have you got your seeds ready, John?" Ma directed the question to Pa as he came in the kitchen door.

At first Pa did not answer. Then he turned around slowly and spoke: "I was wondering whether it's worth the trouble."

Ma was speechless. Joe and John looked as though they couldn't believe, either, what Pa was saying.

"I don't mean the blessing," Pa added hastily. "I mean, is it worth planting at all?"

Ma still could not say a word.

"I've been thinking of what we talked about the other day," continued Pa. "Maybe we should give up the farm and move to town."

Annie gasped. "Give up the farm? Where would we live?"

"Hush, Annie!" Ma found her voice at last. "There's nothing to worry about." She glanced at Pa with a secret kind of look and then spoke quietly. "I thought we had settled that once and for all, John."

"Yes, I know," said Pa. "But I just got to thinking today about all the work for you, now that . . . well, you know, now that another's coming."

"Never mind," said Ma quietly. "We'll manage somehow. It's too late now to start looking for town work. That would be too risky. Let me pack the seeds together and you get ready for church. We can talk more about it afterwards. Little pitchers have big ears."

Annie knew that meant the children were listening to things Ma and Pa did not want them to hear. It was the first time she had heard them talking about leaving the farm. How could they leave? Who would take care of the

9

cows and the pigs, the horses, the chickens and geese, the dogs and the cats? And what was that about some-body coming? Were they going to have company? She wanted to ask these questions aloud but she did not dare.

Pa directed the horses and buggy down to the main valley road. It was called Latsch Valley Road, but there were so many curves and twists that Annie always said to herself: "I think it should be called Winding Valley Road." Around each bend was another farm, and in some of the farmyards she could see horse-drawn buggies and people ready to climb into them. Everyone in the valley went to church on Rogation Day.

During the long ride to Pine Creek Ma and Pa did not say much to each other. They pulled up to the church and Joe jumped down, ready to hitch the horses to one of the posts. Other families were coming from all directions, each carrying baskets or small sacks of seeds.

They filed into church and sat down in their pew. Sitting in the front rows were the fourth- and fifth-grade girls, wearing white dresses and holding baskets of leaves and pussy willows. Before long, the priest came out, preceded by the altar boys and two deacons. Everyone stood up, and the priest started to sing the Litany of the Saints, rolling the Latin phrases off his tongue as easily as if he were speaking English or Polish.

"*Sancta Maria*," chanted Father Gara.

Down the steps marched two altar boys, and behind them came the girls in their white dresses, the deacons, more altar boys, and then Father Gara. Row by row, the people filed out of the pews and joined in the procession, answering the priest in the chant of the litany.

Annie could not understand any of it, but it sounded beautiful. Ma, Pa, and Sally followed the words in their

prayer books that had Latin on one side of the page and Polish on the opposite. They knew when to say *"Ora pro nobis,"* or *"Liberanos, Domine,"* or *"Te rogamos, audinos."*

Around the outside of the church they went and up to the fields behind the Wnuks' house. There they stopped and Father Gara sprinkled holy water in all directions, while everyone held up their seeds. Then they marched back to the church, singing a hymn in Polish.

"I like this a lot better than just sitting in church," thought Annie. "I wish we could march around every Sunday."

Father Gara finished the Mass and everyone moved

slowly out to the big space in front of the high stone steps. In winter, the families hurried quickly to their buggies and set off for their homes as fast as they could. But in nice weather, they stayed for a while and chatted or exchanged the news.

As her parents walked slowly down the steps, Annie could see, just ahead of them, the Pellowski family, who were their neighbors on the farm to the east. They had even more children in their family than Annie had in hers. There they all were, standing in a circle around their parents: Effie, Zenon, Emil, Damazy, Vic, Florian, Daniel and the baby, Julius, who had just learned to walk. Annie did not know exactly how old they all were, except for Vic. He was the same age as she was and they would be in first grade together in the fall.

Mr. Pellowski turned to Pa and Ma as they reached the bottom of the steps.

"Hello, John! Hello, Anna! How goes it? Stop a minute—Mary and I want to ask you something."

"Hello, Barney! Hello, Mary!" Ma and Pa exchanged greetings and then Barney continued.

"Say, we thought tomorrow would be a good day to celebrate Old Frank's birthday. He was eighty in January, you know, but the weather was so bad no one could get up to our place. Then, before we knew it, Lent was here and we had to put off the celebration."

Annie knew that Old Frank was Barney's father. He was the oldest person in the valley and he had come from Poland a long time ago to homestead on the first farm there.

"Why sure, we'll be glad to come, won't we?" answered Pa, and he turned to Ma; she nodded her head in agreement.

"My sister Anna will be coming from Winona with her children, and so will Anton and his family. Jake and Young Frank and the others from around here will probably all show up. Hey, there's Pauline. I want to catch her before she leaves," said Barney as he moved off with Pa toward a tall, dark-haired lady.

"Isn't that Mrs. Jereczek, Ma?" asked Annie.

"Yes, but she's Barney's sister and one of Old Frank's daughters, too," answered Ma.

Annie looked at Mrs. Jereczek, who was holding a small boy in her arms. There were eight other children standing close to her.

"Those are my cousins," said Vic. "I have more than forty first cousins," he bragged.

Annie sighed. Vic was lucky. She had only five first cousins and two of them were babies, too young to play with.

Ma chatted with Mary and several other ladies and then Pa came up to her again.

"Time to get going," he said. "If we're going to plant, then I want to get as much done today as I can. Come Joe, John," he called to the boys, who were standing off to one side of the church, laughing and talking with their friends.

They climbed up to the buggy seats, Pa clicked to the horses, and off they went. The April air was as soft and mild as a June morning. On both sides they passed field after field of freshly plowed soil. The earthy smell, the bright sunshine, the party invitation for the next day—everything combined to make them feel good.

"I wish we could go on riding like this forever," thought Annie. But all too soon, they were at the edge of the small town of Dodge, where Ma and Pa bought groceries and sold their cream.

"I'm going to buy a pony of beer," said Pa as he pulled the horses to a stop in front of the tavern. "I told Barney I'd bring some tomorrow."

"All right, but don't linger to have any now," said Ma.

Annie watched as Pa pushed through the swinging doors. She stood up on the back buggy seat and craned her neck, trying to see what was going on inside the tavern.

"Watch out," warned Sally. "You'll fall off if the horses jerk a little bit."

"I want to see inside," pleaded Annie.

"Well, you can't. Children aren't allowed in taverns." Sally spoke as though she did not consider herself a child anymore. She was going to be thirteen in June.

They sat and waited in the bright April sun. Every now and then, someone would go into the tavern, but no one came out. August began to wiggle and twist on Ma's lap, and Leo tried to stand up on the seat, imitating Annie.

"Joe, run in and tell your Pa to hurry up," said Ma.

Joe jumped down from the back of the wagon and ran to the tavern.

"I thought children weren't supposed to go in taverns," protested Annie.

"Joe is a big boy already—almost a man," said Ma calmly.

Pa and Joe came out, carrying a small keg between them. They wedged it into the space between the front and back seats, right by Annie's feet.

"Why do they call it a pony?" Annie wondered aloud.

"I don't exactly know," answered Pa with a short laugh. "I suppose because it is a small size of barrel, just like a pony is a small size of horse."

14

When they got home Pa carried the pony of beer into the milkhouse and put it in the water to keep cool. Then he and the boys went off to plant the seeds of oats and corn that had been blessed. Ma took her seed packets and went out to the garden. The children tagged along.

"Be a good girl and play with your little brothers, while Sally and I get these planted," she said to Annie.

Annie wanted to help with the planting. She liked the small packages of tiny seeds. Some seeds were like black specks of pepper. Others were shaped and colored like the eyes of birds, or like dried petals from miniature flowers. It was always a surprise to see how different each plant looked, after it grew up from its seed.

With a sigh, Annie took Roman and Leo and August over to the woodpile. They liked to play at making fences and barns out of sticks of wood. For the rest of that day they played while Pa and Joe and John planted in the big fields, and Ma and Sally planted in the garden.

That night, Annie fell asleep thinking of all the tiny kernels and seeds growing in neat rows in the ground.

"Now Ma and Pa won't leave the farm," she whispered to herself, just before sleep came over her like a feather quilt.

Horseless Buggy Rides

On Sunday they hurried home from Mass, and after eating breakfast, finished up the morning chores. Then Pa went to get the pony of beer from the milkhouse, and Ma wrapped two loaves of bread and a coffee cake in a clean cloth.

Once again they settled themselves in their places on the buggy and set off. Down to the valley road they rolled, then left, to the east, around the curve, and up the hill to the Pellowski homestead. There were already three buggies standing in the yard. Next to one of them stood a woman dressed in black, and behind her were two boys and a girl.

"Well, look who's here," Pa called out in Polish to the woman as he directed the team to a spot next to the other buggies. Pa jumped out, handed the reins to Joe, and helped Ma step down.

"I haven't seen you in a long time, Anna," said Pa to the lady in black.

"Not another Anna," thought Annie. There were so many Annas in her family it was hard to keep track of them all. Pa must have known what Annie was thinking because he said: "Annie, here's another Anna. She's the one I used to play with when we were young. I guess she couldn't stand living near to us any longer, so she got married to Joe Olszewski and moved to town."

"Go on with you. Still up to your fooling ways, I see," laughed Mrs. Olszewski.

Annie looked around while Pa joked some more with Ma and the lady. She could not see any man standing near the wagon. Where was Mr. Olszewski?

Suddenly Pa turned serious.

"Must be kind of hard on you with Joe gone. And his father died last year, too, didn't he?"

"Yes, now I've got only my boys and Helen. But we manage all right." Mrs. Olszewski put one arm over her daughter's shoulder and another around one of her sons. Annie could see they felt embarrassed.

"But *your* father is still going strong. I never did see the like. Eighty and still working hard every day."

Before Mrs. Olszewski could reply, another buggy pulled into the yard. It was full of grown-ups and children sitting cramped together.

"Here's Jake and Frances! I declare, we'll never get in to pay our respects to Father if this keeps up." Mrs. Olszewski shook her head but Annie could tell she was happy to see them.

The newly arrived buggy jiggled and bounced as each of its occupants jumped out. These were more of Vic's cousins. Annie knew some of the children by name, but the tall older girls she could never keep straight. Alex and Martin were in John's classroom at school, and Stance was supposed to start first grade in the fall, just as she would. Felix was the same age as Joe and he didn't go to school anymore, either. Emeline was four, just like Leo, and the baby was called Sophie.

The boys started to run for the barn, following Joe, who had unhitched the horses. Annie was about to run after them when Jake called them back.

"What do you mean, running off like that? You go in first and pay your respects to Grandfather, you hear?"

Annie knew that she was expected to do the same, even though Old Frank was not related to her. She would have to go in, wait her turn, and then shake Old Frank's hand and say in Polish: "May God grant you a long life." It seemed funny to her to have to say that because Old Frank had already had a long life. But that was what everyone said.

It took almost an hour for all of the families to pass through the front parlor where Old Frank was sitting. By the time she had at last paid her respects, Annie was hungry. She followed her mother to the kitchen, hoping to get a bit of something to eat.

"Go out and play with the others," said Ma. "You will have to wait for a later sitting before it's your turn for dinner."

"But I'm hungry, Mother," whispered Annie.

"Oh, all right, you can have a piece of bread and butter to last you till then," agreed Ma. "But go off and eat it in a corner, or before you know it, all the children will be here pestering for some."

Annie ate her bread and butter quickly, and then went outside. In different parts of the yard and barns small groups of men, boys and girls stood around talking. She wandered from one to the next, listening and watching. There wasn't enough time to start any games before dinner. Besides, some of the cousins were still shy with each other, getting reacquainted after not having visited the farm for a year.

Soon the first group of people were called in to eat; a half-hour later the second batch of twenty went in. When it was time for the third sitting, Annie heard her mother call.

"Your turn now. Find Sally and the boys and tell them to come in, too."

The table was filled with good things to eat: steamed sausages and roast chicken, mashed potatoes and potato dumplings, sauerkraut and dill pickles, dried apple pie and applesauce, poppy seed cake and sugar cookies. When the children had eaten all they could, the ladies who had been working in the kitchen sat down at last and ate their fill. But they did not sit and linger. As soon as their plates were empty, they gathered them up and took them to the kitchen to wash. When all the dishes were done and the table cleared for the last time, the men sat down around it.

"What will it be, Father, sheepshead or euchre?" asked Barney. It's your birthday we're celebrating."

"Then let it be sheepshead," announced Old Frank.

The children watched for two rounds. First Barney shuffled the cards and swiftly dealt them out in turn; when the cards were all played out, it was Pa's turn to deal. Every time it was possible for him to trump a trick, he always put his card down with a thump of his fist.

"Now I've got you," Pa would say. But sometimes one

19

of the other men trumped higher. Then Pa would shake his head and look unhappy.

"I'm going outside," announced Damazy. "It's no fun just watching them play." Four of his brothers and four cousins followed him immediately. Then Joe and John went out and finally the Olszewski boys slipped away, too. Annie wanted to go and see what they were doing.

"Sally, let's go outside," whispered Annie.

"No. I want to stay inside," insisted Sally. She liked to listen to the talk of the married ladies and the older girls.

"Then I'll be the only girl out there," complained Annie loudly.

"That doesn't matter," said Ma. "Take Roman out for a walk around the yard. Sally has to help Effie and Helen put the little ones down for their naps."

Annie slipped on her coat and helped Roman button his jacket. They stepped out into the yard and looked around. Over by the buggies they could see the thirteen boys. Their voices were loud and bragging. Annie and Roman walked closer to listen.

"I *know* our buggy is faster than the others," she heard her brother Joe saying. "Can't you see? The wheels are bigger."

"What's that got to do with it?" Alex wanted to know.

"Can't you figure it out?" Joe's voice was full of confidence. "Bigger wheels cover more ground each time they go around, so they are bound to be faster."

"That don't sound right to me," said Alex. "I think it's the horses pulling the buggy that make it go slow or fast."

"Yah, I think so, too," agreed Zenon. He was Vic and Damazy's oldest brother. Vic nodded his head, backing him up.

"Well, sure, horses do make a difference," admitted

Joe. "But I'm talking about the buggies by themselves. I'll bet if they were all lined up at the top of the hill and then if we gave them a push, ours would go down faster." He glanced over to the incline that banked steeply to one side of the dugway road. All the boys swerved their eyes in the same direction.

"That's a nice, smooth hill," said John. "I bet our buggy would go down faster than a jackrabbit."

"Not any faster than ours," said Zenon.

"Come on, let's prove it to them," said Vic. He picked up the tongue and steered his family's buggy in the direction of the hill. Zenon and his other brothers pushed it from behind.

"Well, scaredy-cats, are you afraid to prove it?" Vic taunted Joe and John.

Annie saw her brothers hesitate for a moment. Then they started pushing their buggy over to the hill, lining it up carefully next to the one already there. Pulling Roman along by the hand, she ran to Joe and John.

"Pa won't like it if you wreck the buggy," she said.

"Who's going to wreck it? We're just going to prove ours is faster, that's all," Joe assured her. He climbed up to the driver's seat and John tilted the tongue backwards so Joe could steer with it. Zenon did the same and then his four brothers got behind, ready to give a push.

"That's no fair," cried Joe. "You'll get a head start. One to steer and one to push is all we need. Felix, you count to three and then we're off."

"One, two, three!" Felix shouted.

Zenon steered while Damazy pushed his buggy and Joe steered while John gave him a shove. Down the hill went the buggies, gathering speed as they went.

"Faster, Zenon, faster! Pull her straight," yelled Vic.

Annie held her breath at first. She knew Joe and John

were not supposed to be playing with the buggy, but in the excitement of the race, she forgot all about that.

"Go, Joe, go!" she shrieked.

"Go, Joe, go!" Roman imitated her, hopping up and down in excitement.

The buggies reached the bottom of the hill at almost the same moment and then kept moving forward onto the flat stretch of road where they came to a stop. They were not more than a few feet apart; Joe was in front, but not by much.

"I told you ours would go faster," bragged Joe.

"You didn't go any faster than I did," said Zenon. "We got here at the same time only my buggy stopped a little sooner. Probably there was a stone in the road."

They argued back and forth for a bit while the others raced down the hill to see the results.

"Looks like a tie," said Alex. No one said anything to that. They got behind the buggies and pulled and pushed them up the dugway and around to the farmyard.

"I still can't figure it out," said Joe. "Ours should have gone faster." Just then, he looked at the wheels of one of the other buggies in the line. "These are a *lot* smaller than ours. I'll bet we'd beat this one by a mile."

"You're never going to find out if you could, because that's ours," said Felix. "Our Pa would whip us good if he found us playing around with it."

"We're not playing around," argued Joe. "We're testing them out. Your Pa would certainly want to know if bigger wheels are faster, so he could get some—right? Come on, try it just once."

"I'll push you," said Alex, eagerly. He wanted to see how his older brother would do in a race.

"Come on, Felix," begged the other boys. "We'll push it right back up the hill for you." Felix reluctantly gave in.

They lined up the buggies at the top of the hill. Joe and John readied themselves, and so did Felix and Alex. Zenon counted out: "One, two, three, go!"

Again the buggies started down slowly and picked up speed only when they were more than halfway down the hill.

"Come on Felix! Let her go!" shouted Alex.

"Go, Joe, go!" yelled Annie and Roman and John.

All the way down they were wheel to wheel. They came to a stop in almost the exact spot where the first race had ended. Joe's buggy was again a little ahead, but by no more than a foot. He was shaking his head when the others came running up.

"I just don't get it. No matter what size the wheels are, the buggies all come down at the same speed."

"I told you it was the horses pulling that makes the speed," said Alex.

23

They lined up behind the buggies and started pushing them back up the dugway road.

"I'm tired of pushing uphill," said Vic. "I want a ride *down* the hill."

"Me, too," said Damazy. All the younger boys agreed they should have a ride downhill; Annie wanted one, too, but she was afraid to say so aloud. The boys might not let her ride along.

"I have it," cried Joe. "We'll line up all four buggies at the top, load each one with the same number of people, and then see how fast they go. That will be the real test. If they all stop at the same spot, more or less, it means the wheel size makes no difference."

They pushed the buggies back up, and this time the Olszewski boys lined up their buggy right next to the one Joe was steering. Without saying a word, Annie lifted Roman up to the back seat behind Joe, and then climbed up herself. Alex put his two younger brothers up on one side of the seat behind Felix, and then got ready to push.

"I'll jump on after we start moving," he said.

"Oh, good, I can do that, too," said John and he motioned to Annie and Roman to make room for him.

Vic and his younger brother climbed up behind Zenon, leaving room for Damazy.

"Where does that leave me?" complained Emil. He was only a year younger than Zenon, and had been standing off to one side up until then.

"You go with the Olszewski boys—that will just about even out the weight," said Zenon.

"Now remember," warned Joe. "Steer straight ahead so we don't lock wheels."

Nervously, Annie looked to each side. On the left, Felix had positioned the buggy at quite a distance. But on the right, the Olszewski buggy looked awfully close. She could almost reach out and touch it. She was just about to say something when Joe called out: "One, two, three, go!"

From behind, the four boys each gave a mighty push and then, before the buggies were moving fast, they jumped up into the back seats. At first, everything seemed to move very slowly. Annie looked down the steep hill to the bottom. She felt a funny tickle in her middle, just like the feeling she got at the top of the hay barn, before sliding down to the bottom.

Suddenly the buggies began to pick up speed. It felt so strange to be moving along, without any horses in front. Faster and faster turned the wheels. It made Annie dizzy to look at them. She clutched Roman as he yelled: "Go, Joe, go!"

Off to her right, Annie saw Edward Olszewski, hanging on to the wagon tongue for dear life. All at once, the tongue swerved to the side. The Olszewski buggy started coming closer to their buggy.

"Pull her right!" screamed Joe at Edward.

Edward tried to straighten out the tongue but it was all he could do to keep it from moving further off to the left. His buggy came closer and closer. Stiff with fright, Annie watched the hub of one wheel inch closer to the hub of the wheel just below her seat. The buggy gave a slight jolt as the two hubs touched. Then they were pressed tightly together as though locked with a bolt. They stopped turning and started scraping the grassy hillside.

"Screeeeeeech!" The wheels squealed as they slid over the grass. "Ping!" A piece of metal snapped.

A shout made Annie look up. The Olszewski buggy was veering off to the right, away from her.

"Thank goodness," she thought. "They are moving away from us." But at that moment she glanced down at the wheel again. There was still a second wheel attached to it, locked tight at the hub!

"You lost your wheel," screamed Annie, but it was already too late. They knew they had lost their wheel because their buggy gave a dip and bump and then came to a sudden stop. The three boys went sailing through the air. With a thump! thump! thump! they landed on the grassy slope one right after the other, and almost on top of each other.

26

Annie looked back, trying to see if they were hurt, but the buggy she was in was going so fast she could hardly turn around. At last they reached the bottom and Joe steered the buggy to a standstill. The buggies to the left of them continued for a few more yards, because they had no extra wheel to slow them down.

All the boys were silent as they jumped down. Shakily, Annie climbed down, too, and ran to where Emil and the Olszewski boys were sitting on the grass, dazed and speechless.

"Are you hurt?" she asked.

"No," answered Edward, "but what about our buggy?" He looked really worried as he got up slowly and walked unsteadily to where the buggy stood, minus its wheel. The other boys were already crowding around it.

"Well, at least the axle didn't get broken," said Joe. He was trying to sound cheerful. "We should be able to get it fixed in no time. All we need is a nut and maybe a washer. We should be able to find the nut near the spot where the wheels locked."

They spread out over the hillside, searching the grass carefully.

"I think I remember where it happened," said Annie. "I was closest to that wheel." She climbed to a spot halfway up the hill and looked for the place where the skid marks started. Just below them, she began to search the ground closely. The grass grew in knobby clumps. Each time she saw a dark spot from a few feet away it would look like a metal nut but as soon as she looked more carefully, it would turn out to be a chunk of earth or a dead leaf. The boys were starting to give up and Annie was just about ready to do the same when she spotted a funny shape sticking up from a cluster of dandelion leaves. Could it be? Yes, it was!

"I found it! I found it!" she shrieked, jumping up and down.

"Are you fooling?" Joe asked, looking at her severely.

"No, honest, I found it. Here it is." Annie held up the nut in the palm of her hand.

The boys came forward slowly, not quite ready to believe she had it.

"That's it!" cried John. "She really did find it."

"Then let's get our buggy fixed," said Edward. He was nervously looking up the dugway road, expecting someone to come down it from the house at any moment. If one of his uncles came, he knew he would be in trouble.

While several of the boys lifted up the one side of the buggy, Joe and Edward rolled the loose wheel into place and slipped it onto the axle. They pushed hard until the wheel was in line with the back one.

"Quick, put it on!" cried Joe, and one of the boys tried to screw the nut tightly on to the pin sticking out from the axle. It would only go on part way, and the wheel still wobbled when they tried to move the buggy.

"We need a washer, and some pliers to tighten the nut," said Zenon. "Vic, run and get them from the tool shed."

While Vic was gone, the boys tried to turn and twist the nut with their fingers, but they could not get it to tighten up closely to the hub.

"Are you sure that's the right nut?" asked Edward.

"It's gotta be," answered Joe. "None of the other buggies lost a wheel." Just to be sure they looked carefully at all the wheels on all the buggies. None were missing a nut.

"Here," cried Vic, panting as he ran up and thrust a pair of pliers at Zenon. "I brought a washer, too, just in case."

Zenon unscrewed the nut, slipped the washer onto the pin, and then grasped the nut tightly with the pliers. He turned and turned and at last got the washer and nut to fit snugly against the wood of the hub. Now the wheel turned smoothly and evenly, just as it had before.

"Hurray!" they all shouted.

"We'd better get them back up to the yard," said Alex. "That card game won't last much longer. It will be time to go home for milking soon."

Grunting and complaining, they pushed the wagons up the road. They were just backing them into the spaces along the barn, where they had been before, when Annie saw Pa headed their way. Behind him were Mrs. Olszewski and Helen, Jake and some of the other grown-ups.

"What are you monkeying around with those buggies for?" asked Pa. "Have you been up to something?"

There was complete silence among the boys. Annie hoped Pa would not ask her what they had been doing. She would have to answer truthfully.

"Now, John, don't get your dander up," laughed Mrs. Olszewski. "Don't you remember the mischief we used to get into? There's nothing wrong with the buggies, as far as I can see. Come boys, it's time we headed back. Winona is a long way off."

"Am I ever glad their buggy is fixed again," thought Annie as she breathed a sigh of relief. Joe must have thought so, too, because he gave her arm a squeeze.

Father Had a Little Lamb

"I have to go to Father's place tomorrow to shear the sheep," announced Pa one evening at supper. "I'll need some help."

Joe and John were silent. They knew their job, if they went, would be to catch and hold down the smelly, wriggling sheep. It was not a job they liked.

"I'll go," offered Annie.

"You! Why, you couldn't hold down a sheep's tail," scoffed John.

Annie knew that he was trying to make fun of her, because Grandfather's sheep had no tails. She pretended not to notice his comment.

"I can mind the lambs while you do the shearing, Pa," offered Annie. Secretly, that was really why she wanted to go. She loved watching the frolics of the baby lambs. They jumped and kicked and butted each other so playfully that it was fun to tend them when they were so young. It would not seem at all like work to her.

"I guess you could be a help at that," admitted Pa. Then he looked at the boys. "Joe, you'll come along with us, too. If we get an early start we'll be finished before dinnertime."

The next morning, Annie got up as soon as she heard Sally stirring. It was barely light outside.

"What are you getting up so early for?" mumbled Sally sleepily. Now that school was out, she liked to stay a little longer in bed each morning.

"Don't you remember?" asked Annie in exasperation. "I'm going with Pa to Grandfather's, to help with the sheep shearing. Pa said he wants to get an early start."

"Not as early as this," groaned Sally. "He has to do the milking first. And he won't leave without breakfast. Come back to bed for a while."

"No, I'm going to help with the milking," answered Annie.

"I suppose I'd better get up and start breakfast, then, if you're in so much of a hurry to get going." Sally slid out of bed and started to get dressed.

The door at the bottom of the stairs opened, and they heard Ma calling softly:

"Sally! Sally! Are you up?"

"Yes, Ma. What is it?" Sally whispered so as not to wake the younger boys sleeping in the next room.

"I want you to go milking for me," answered Ma. "I'll make breakfast." She moved away from the door.

31

Annie looked at Sally, wondering what she was thinking. Usually Ma helped Pa and Joe with the milking, while John fed the calves and did other chores. For almost as long as Annie could remember, it was Sally who had made breakfast and helped Roman, Leo and August get dressed. But lately, Ma often asked Sally to milk in her place.

Sally had a worried look on her face.

"Ma isn't sick, is she?" asked Annie. She didn't like it when Ma had to stay in bed, like the time last year when baby Jacob died, soon after he was born. It made Ma so sad and tired. Annie wanted Ma to be cheerful and happy, the way she usually was.

"No, she isn't sick," answered Sally thoughtfully. "She just wants a change now and then."

Annie wanted to ask Sally if she had heard Ma and Pa talk any more about leaving the farm, but she was afraid to. "Better not," she thought. "That might make Sally remind them about it."

"I'll go down and help with breakfast," she said aloud. She crept down carefully in the early morning darkness, taking care not to stumble on the steep stairs.

There was no one in the kitchen. Ma must have gone back to bed. Or maybe she was getting dressed. Annie went to the pantry and brought out a big hunk of bacon. Wielding the big butcher knife, she was about to start slicing when Sally came down.

"You can't do that," protested Sally. "You'll cut yourself for sure."

"I want to help," said Annie. "Can't you cut a few slices so I can start frying them?"

"Ma will be up in a little while. You wait until then to see if she wants to have bacon. Start setting the table if you want to do something." She opened the door and walked off quickly to the barn.

Annie set out cups, plates, knives, forks and spoons. She put the sugar bowl in the middle of the table, and next to it a small bowl of butter. Then there was nothing to do but wait.

At last Ma came into the kitchen. Without saying a word she sliced bacon and put it in the frying pan.

"I'll watch it for you, Ma," offered Annie.

Ma smiled. "You can't hardly reach the top of the stove."

"I could stand on a chair," said Annie.

"Well, all right." Ma pushed a chair near to the stove, but not too close. Handing Annie the long-handled fork, she showed her how to keep turning the thick slices of bacon so they would get crisp but not burned. Then she put water in a pot and set it over the hottest part of the stove, to boil for oatmeal. After cutting a whole loaf of bread into thick slices, she began to break eggs in a bowl.

Annie cautiously turned the slices. The hot fat spit at her, landing in droplets on her hands and arms. It hurt for a second but as soon as she rubbed the spots the pain went away. The smoke pinched her eyes so that she had to blink hard to see. She didn't complain, though, because she wanted so much to help.

From the ceiling overhead came the sound of soft thumps and scratches.

"The boys are up," said Ma, coming over to look at the bacon. "That looks done. Can you go up and get them dressed?"

By the time Annie had finished helping them, John and Sally were back in the kitchen, and Pa and Joe followed soon after. They ate breakfast quickly and soon were on their way to Near Grandfather's farm. Pa's mother and father lived only two farms away, down in the same valley, so they called them Near Grandmother and Grandfather. Ma's mother and father lived in Winona, a long ways away, so they were called Far Grandmother and Grandfather.

"Pa, how come we don't have any sheep?" asked Annie as they rode along the valley road.

"That's a long story," said Pa with a laugh. "I don't like sheep. They caused me lots of trouble when I was a boy."

At first Annie made no comment. Whenever Pa talked about the time he was a boy, she tried to imagine what he had looked like. But no matter how hard she tried, Pa always looked like Pa in her mind. Still, she enjoyed it when he or Ma told about the things they did when they were little.

"What kind of trouble?" asked Annie finally.

"All kinds. Sheep are stubborn and have a mind of their own. They like to go where they want to instead of where they are supposed to. And never turn your back on them—they can butt you hard, where it hurts." Pa gave Annie a light spank on her bottom, to show where he meant.

"But not the lambs, Pa. They don't butt people."

"Oh, yes they do," contradicted Pa. "I remember, one time, I had to take our flock over to the Olszewski's. Anna and Barney brought theirs, too. We used to take turns watching them. We had the devil of a time that day. They just wouldn't stay put in one flock. Every time we tried to go home and leave them with John Olszewski, they'd scatter in all directions, or start following us back. There was one lamb in particular—he was a real nuisance. From the time he was born he just followed me like a shadow. Wherever I went, he wanted to go."

"Just like the song, Pa," giggled Annie. She couldn't resist singing it in a new way:

> Father had a little lamb, little lamb, little lamb;
> Father had a little lamb; its fleece was white as
> snow.

> And everywhere that Father went, Father went,
> Father went;
> And everywhere that Father went, the lamb
> was sure to go.

> It followed him to school one day, school one
> day, school one day;
> It followed him to school one day, which was
> against the rule.

"He would have followed me to school if I'd gone," agreed Pa. "But I was too busy helping Father. That day, I knew he wanted me to come back as soon as I could to help with the corn hoeing. We could not get those sheep to stay put. It was hot as blazes and we were huffing and puffing like steam engines from all that chasing. I went down to the spring to get a drink of water and darned if that lamb didn't follow me. Only I didn't see him. I was leaning over, taking a good, long drink, when he gave me a butt in the rear end—I tumbled right down into the creek."

"Oh, Pa, did you get hurt?" asked Annie. She tried to be serious but she could not help laughing.

"No, not then," replied Pa. "But when I got back to Father, he took the strap to me and then I did feel it. He thought we'd been swimming in the creek and wouldn't stand for fooling around when there was so much work to be done. He didn't give me time to explain."

It was so hard to imagine Pa being spanked. Annie tried to picture it all the rest of the way to Grandfather's.

They arrived at the farm and after saying "Hello" to Grandmother in the kitchen, Pa and Joe set right to work with Grandfather. A few yards away from the sheep shed and pen they placed a large wooden tub and then filled it with water. Pa poured a liquid from a bottle into the water. It smelled strong and sharp. Off to another side of the pen, Joe and Grandfather set a platform of wood. Then Pa picked up his shears.

"I'm ready," he announced. "Bring on the first one."

Grandfather and Joe went into the pen and separated one ewe from the rest of the flock. They guided her out through the gate, with her lamb following right behind her. Pa took a firm hold of the ewe around the neck and front legs.

"Hold on to the lamb, Anienka. Make sure it doesn't go out of sight or bleat for its mother. She'll stand still if she can see her baby is near."

Annie cuddled the lamb in her arms. Its soft, white fleece felt almost silky under her fingers. It smelled like fresh milk.

Pa started shearing the ewe, snipping carefully all around her neck. The wool didn't fall off, but stayed in one piece. Annie watched, holding on tightly to the lamb.

"Baaaaa," bleated the lamb as it struggled to leave her arms. It tried to move closer to its mother.

"Maaaaa," blatted the mother ewe in answer, attempting to jump over Pa's legs to get to her baby.

"Let her get closer. Don't hold so tight," said Pa. His long, sharp shears kept snip-snipping at the ewe's thick coat, which was now folded back halfway across her flanks.

Annie loosened her hold and let the lamb nuzzle its mother for a few minutes. In the pen, Grandfather and Joe struggled to separate another ewe from the flock. At last, they caught one near the gate and guided her out to Pa. A few more minutes and Pa was finished with the first ewe. He exchanged ewes with Grandfather and started snipping at the second one. Joe helped Grandfather lift the first one and dip it into the big wooden tub of disinfectant.

Now Annie had two lambs to watch out for. She had to make sure they did not get too close to Pa's shears or the dipping tub. Soon the dipping was completed and the mother ewe was helped out of the tub. Off she trotted, with her lamb moving cautiously behind her, as though it could not believe this funny-looking, shorn creature was its mother. Annie laughed so hard she almost fell over backwards. The second lamb leaped away, running to play with the first one.

"Maaaaa," complained the second ewe, still being shorn by Pa's flashing shears.

"Bring her lamb back," cried Pa. "Otherwise she's not likely to stand still. And be more careful after this."

Annie tugged at the lamb, but it would not come back.

"I'll have to carry you, then," she said, lifting the lamb in her arms. She staggered with it back to the place where Pa was shearing.

For two hours they kept up the same routine. Pa would shear, then turn the ewe over to Grandfather and Joe for dipping. As soon as they completed the dipping, they went into the pen to get another ewe. Annie did her best to keep the lambs where they would not get in the way, and yet would still be in sight of their mothers. At last, all the ewes with lambs were done.

"Now we have only those three ewes left that haven't dropped their lambs yet, and the ram," said Pa. "You can go and play with the lambs all you want. Just keep them away from here."

Annie ran to the flock of ewes and lambs. They had moved to a small meadow below the barn and were grazing. Now that the lambs were all safe and secure near their mothers, they gamboled and playfully butted each other, tumbling in heaps on the fresh spring grass and then jumping up for more of the same.

She ducked her head, pretending to rush toward one of the lambs as if to butt it. The lamb lowered its head and took a determined run in Annie's direction. Just before it reached her, she jumped aside and the lamb bumped its head against thin air, fell on its face, and did a kind of half-somersault.

"Ha! Ha! I fooled you," laughed Annie.

The lamb looked at her, puzzled, and once again lowered its head, running towards her as fast as its spindly legs could move. Once more she lowered her own head and faced the lamb, jumping out of the way just in time. Giggling and laughing, Annie played the mock-butting game over and over, sometimes with the same lamb, sometimes with others. Suddenly, she noticed two of them, about to rush her at the same time.

"You think two of you can bring me down, do you?" taunted Annie, as both of them lowered their heads and prepared to rush her. She hunched her shoulders down, leaned her head forward, and put her weight on one foot, preparing to jump out of the way quickly. Off to her left she could see a fresh cow pie.

"I don't want to land in that direction," she thought. "I'd better jump off to the right this time." As she was shifting her weight to the other foot, she saw, out of the corner of her eye, a movement in back of her. She half-turned but by then it was too late. One of the other lambs, coming from behind, butted her firmly and swiftly. She lost her balance and fell to the left, arms outstretched to stop her fall.

Splat! Her body landed short of the cow pie but her hands and arms came to rest right in the middle of the smelly, gooey mess.

Annie did not know whether to laugh or cry. She knew she couldn't blame the lambs; they were playing in the only way they knew how. And hadn't Pa warned her never to turn her back on them? She rubbed her hands and arms against some fresh grass, hoping to clean off the sticky mess.

"I'd better go to the pump and wash it off," she thought. She hurried up the meadow, past the barn, and across the yard, holding her hands and arms behind her.

"I hope Pa and Joe and Grandfather don't see me," she thought.

Joe was standing around, waiting for Pa to finish shearing the ram. He looked at Annie as she tried to walk past, turned sideways, arms behind her back.

"What you got there?" he asked.

"Nothing." Annie ran to the pump and started to prime it.

Joe came hurrying up and saw the brown, sticky mess on her arms and hands. "Let me do that," he said with a laugh, taking hold of the pump handle. "What did those lambs do to you?"

Annie blushed. "Nothing. I just fell."

"Mighty unlucky place to fall." Joe grinned as Annie scrubbed her hands and arms under the clear water that now gushed from the pump.

Annie smiled back at him sweetly. She would never tell what had happened.

"I guess that's it," called out Pa as he and Grandfather finished dipping the ram. They both came to give their hands a good scrubbing. Then they splashed the cool water on their faces, and each took a long drink, using the dipper hanging on the top of the pump.

Grandmother stepped out from the kitchen door.

"Sure you won't stay for dinner?" she called.

"No," answered Pa. "We have to get back. After you've picked out the fleeces you want to keep for spinning, I'll come back and help Father bundle up the rest of the wool to sell." He packed up his tools and they jumped up on the buggy, and started toward home.

"Did you like playing with those lambs?" Pa asked. "Would you still like to have some of your own?"

"I think she's had enough of lambs for a while," interrupted Joe with a laugh. "They gave her a dose of not-so-nice medicine. Yes, a nice, sticky salve for her arms. Haw! Haw!"

"I have *not* had enough of lambs," protested Annie. "Just you wait and see. When I grow up, I'm going to have my own to take care of, and I won't let anyone else near them."

"Fine by me," laughed Joe.

"Suits me fine, too," agreed Pa.

"They'll see, I'm going to do just that," Annie assured herself silently. It was no use talking about it any more with Joe. All he would do was make fun of her. "But I'd better watch Pa carefully next year, to see how he does the shearing," she thought. "And maybe I'll have only two lambs, so I can always watch them." She started picturing them in her mind, two frisky lambs, butting and jumping in the pasture, and smiled all the way home, thinking about them.

Wet Hay

Sssss-screeech! Sssss-screeech! The scraping, grating sound of steel on stone filled Annie's ears as she turned the crank of the grindstone. Pa was sharpening the sickles of his hay mower, and she and John were taking turns helping him. One poured water while the other turned the wheel. They had to keep the handle going around at a firm, steady speed and not slow down when Pa held the small, triangle-shaped sickles against the edge of the stone. It made a terrible noise that hurt the ears. Annie always gritted her teeth when she was cranking the grindstone for Pa.

"That about does it," said Pa. "Now I can put them

back in the mower and get to work cutting the hay." Going up to the hay mower, he slipped a pair of sickles into the correct slots and fitted in the screws, tightening them as much as he could. The rest of the mower looked like a giant mouth missing half of its teeth, until Pa had all the sickles back into place. They made a shining, sharp, jagged edge that would cut down the hay swiftly and neatly.

Annie had only seen the mower work once because Pa did not like children around while he mowed the hay.

"Better to be safe than sorry," said Pa. "The sickles are so sharp and go so fast, I'd never be able to stop in time, if someone popped up, sudden-like."

But when the hay was dry and had to be raked over on the other side, she could go along and watch Pa for a while, if she wanted to.

"I sure do hope this good weather holds," said Pa at the dinner table one day, after he had raked all morning. "The hay would be dry enough by tomorrow to bring it in. Barney said he would let me try out his new hayloader. Says you can load up twice as fast with it."

"Why do you have to wait till the hay is so dry, Pa?" asked Annie.

"You don't want our barn to go up in smoke, do you?" laughed Pa.

Annie shook her head, eyes wide in surprise.

"That's what happens when you put wet, green hay in your barn. It gets to steaming and smoking. Pretty soon it catches fire from all that heat. Doesn't even need a match to light it. Then, poof! Up in smoke goes your barn. There's more than one farmer lost a barn that way."

"Are you sure the hay will be dry enough by tomorrow?" asked Annie with a worried look. She did not want their barn to catch fire.

"It will be just fine by noon if we don't get any rain tonight," Pa assured her. "I'm going over to help Barney and Old Frank in the morning and then they'll bring the hayloader over here. We should get both fields done if it works as fast as Barney claims. Father said he'd come and help, too."

"Will they be staying for supper?" Ma wanted to know.

"No, I don't think that will be necessary," said Pa. "But a cool drink and a bite of something sweet might be nice to break the afternoon."

The next morning Pa left early to help the neighbors with their hay. As soon as he was gone, Ma took out the flour and began to stir up a big bowl of dough. When it was smooth and round and plump she covered it with a cloth and set it in the pantry.

"Now while that is rising, we'll make a batch of molasses sugar cookies," said Ma. She stirred up lard and brown sugar and then added eggs and molasses. She beat them until the mixture was smooth and syrupy looking and then put in a lot of flour and a little milk. Last came the baking soda and spices. After sprinkling flour on the table, Ma rolled out a big round of dough.

"Can I cut them out?" asked Annie.

"I'll cut them and put them on the baking sheets and you can sprinkle them with sugar," said Ma. Taking one of her good china cups that had lost its handle, she turned it upside down and dipped the rim in flour. Then she pressed it firmly over the dough, lifted it up, and there was a round cookie. Over and over again she dipped the cup rim in flour and pressed it on the dough. Carefully, she lifted the rounds onto the baking sheets.

"Mind you put just a light sprinkle of sugar on each cookie," said Ma.

In no time at all, the first two sheets were ready to go in the oven and Ma started cutting more cookies. Her cheeks were flushed from the heat.

"Sally, will you punch down the dough for the *pączki* and set it to rise again?" called out Ma. "Annie and I have a cookie factory going and we don't want to stop."

They made dozens of fat, round molasses cookies, plump and brown and smelling so delicious Annie could hardly wait for dinner.

"Here, take one for yourself and one for each of the boys," said Ma. "In a little while you can come back and help me sugar the *pączki*."

Annie took the cookies to the boys and hurried back to the kitchen.

Ma was rolling out the risen dough and cutting it into small squares. She placed them on the baking sheets to rise for a while longer and went to check on the deep, wide kettle of fat getting hotter and hotter on the summer kitchen stove.

"It's hot enough, I think," said Ma after fifteen minutes had gone by. She placed a large bowl on the kitchen table and poured in some sugar. "Be ready to start as soon as the first batch is done," she told Annie.

One by one Ma carefully dropped the squares of dough into the hot fat. They sputtered and crackled so she stepped back quickly. After a few minutes, she flipped each one over. When they were crispy and brown on both sides she lifted them out with a long-handled fork and put them back on the baking sheet.

"Be careful! They are hot," said Ma as she set the sheet down in front of Annie. She went to fry another batch of squares, and Annie set to work. Dropping a square into the sugar, she turned it over until it was coated on all

45

sides, then placed it back on the sheet. Her mouth watered as she handled the *pączki,* so that she had all she could do to keep up. At last they came to the final batch. Ma brought it to Annie and she used up the rest of the sugar, turning the *pączki* this way and that. Then she looked up at Ma expectantly.

"All right," said Ma with a laugh. "It's close to dinnertime but you may have a small one." She selected a crunchy brown square and handed it to Annie.

Annie bit into it. Never had she tasted anything better than Ma's *pączki,* with the crisp, chewy outside and the soft white inside.

Just before noon Pa came back. Ma was ready to set the dinner on the table. Annie did not eat too much meat and potatoes because she knew they would have cookies and *pączki* later.

"Got to hurry," said Pa as he gulped down his milk. "They will be out in the hay field by now. I told them to go there directly."

"I want to see how the hayloader works, Pa," said Annie.

Pa looked at her a moment. "No harm in that, I guess. You can all come out and have a look. But stay clear of the machine. Joe, you bring the team and rack as soon as you can. We'll start loading Barney's rack first."

"I'll have a look when I bring your lunch, John," said Ma. "The boys can come then, too. Is three-thirty all right?"

"Sounds fine to me, Anna," answered Pa.

Annie skipped and ran all the way out to the hay field with Pa. The machine had not yet arrived. She knelt down and felt the hay. It was good and dry. She did not want any wet hay in their barn.

Suddenly they heard a team of horses coming. It rounded the curve and Annie could see the hayloader attached behind the rack; it looked like a tall, narrow stairway or ladder of metal, looming up into the sky. "The hay must go up that stairway," thought Annie.

And that was just how it worked. Now Pa did not have to work so hard throwing up the hay one forkful at a time into the rack. The hayloader picked it up and carried it to the top of the ladder; from there it dropped down into the rack.

"If you want it to go to the front of the rack, you move this lever down," explained Barney.

"What won't they think of next," said Pa admiringly. He and Barney set to work and very soon the rack was almost full of hay.

Annie noticed that Old Frank and Grandfather weren't working by the machine. On the steep, sloping side of the field they were gathering up bundles of hay and binding them together with the longest strands of hay. These bundles they piled on wooden frames shaped like windows without panes. By the time Joe arrived with their own team and rack, Old Frank and Grandfather each had a small haystack on their frames, and Pa and Barney had their rack as full as they could make it.

"You take this rack back and unload it while we work on the next one," said Pa to Joe.

"Oh, goody," cried Annie. "I get to ride back on the top of the load."

"All right, then, up you go," said Pa as he swung Annie up to the top of the loaded hay rack.

"Don't go too fast," she called to Joe. She could see Pa and Barney attaching the empty rack to the hayloader. Off to the side Old Frank and Grandfather were stooping down next to the wooden frames. They picked them up on their backs and, bending low, started walking behind the full rack, heading toward the barn.

"Why don't you bring that hay over here?" called Pa. "No need for you to carry it all the way."

But Old Frank and Grandfather just waved their hands as if to say, "Never mind," and continued trudging slowly toward the barn.

As soon as they got to the barn, Joe helped them lift the wooden frames from their backs and set them flat on the ground. With the giant fork on the pulley, they lifted both stacks up to the hayloft. The hay stayed in a neat, round bundle. Then Old Frank and Grandfather picked up the wooden frames and went back to the hay field.

"How come they carry the hay like that?" asked Annie.

"That's the way they learned in Poland and I guess they still like to do it here. Beats me," said Joe, "when this is so much easier. But I guess it would be pretty dangerous to take the loader down on that slope—it might turn over. I will say this—they can sure stack hay! Better than anybody I know."

Annie went to the house to tell Ma about the exciting new machine.

"It goes so fast!" she exclaimed. "And it shoots the hay just where Pa wants it on the hay rack."

Load after load was brought in from the field. Ma and Sally and John and Joe could hardly keep up with the unloading. At a quarter after three Joe was ready to take one of the empty racks back to the field, but this time, Ma, Sally, John, Annie and the little boys all climbed aboard carrying baskets of food, jars of cool milk and buttermilk, and a tin pot of hot coffee.

The men in the field had their rack full of hay, ready to take to the barn. In the shadow of the full hay rack, right in the middle of the hay field, they all sat down to a picnic lunch. How good everything tasted, with the sweet smell of the hay surrounding them. Annie would have liked to sit there for the rest of the afternoon.

"Back to work," said Pa, speaking in Polish. "I don't know why, but I don't like the look of the sky back there in the southwest. What do you say?" Pa turned to Old Frank. He looked at the sky a moment.

"It will rain by seven," was all he said.

"We should be done long before then, if you and Sally can do the milking, Anna. How about it?" asked Pa.

"We can manage," said Ma quietly.

They all rode back on the top of the hay rack, laughing and giggling. Then it was time to do all the chores: carry in wood, feed the chickens, geese and pigs, get the cows, start the supper. Whenever Joe came back with a full load of hay, John and Annie had to run to the haymow to help spread the clumps as they dropped down from the fork.

Annie was in the haymow, frantically moving the hay by armfuls to the furthest corners, when it got so dark she could hardly see. Joe had already left with the rack, and John was helping in the barn.

Crack! Boom, boom, boom, boom! A fork of lightning was followed by a tremendous burst of thunder. Annie scurried down the ladder to the lower barn. Ma was lighting the lantern. It was only six o'clock, but it was as dark as night.

"I do wish Joe hadn't gone out again," said Ma.

"He said it would be the last load," John assured her.

"Let's hurry and get the rest of the cows milked, then, so we can help him unload quickly."

Ma and Sally and John each began to milk a cow, while Annie and her younger brothers fed the kittens by pouring milk into shallow pans. The lightning began to flash and crackle more frequently. Ma was just finishing up the last cow when they heard Joe come back with the load of hay.

"Run and help him unload," urged Ma. "You, too, Annie. I'll watch the boys."

As Annie stepped out of the barn, she felt a drop of rain fall on her arm. "It's raining," she cried. Now the hay would get wet before they could put it in the barn.

"A sprinkle or two like that won't hurt," said John. "If only it doesn't rain harder."

Quickly, he and Joe attached the whippletree to the pulley rope and then Joe jabbed the fork deep into the hay. Annie and Sally waited in the haymow.

"I'm just going to see if it is really dry," said Annie as she grabbed an armful of hay from the first bundle that dropped down. It did feel warm and dry, and she was relieved. Sally used a pitchfork to spread the hay on one side, but that was too dangerous for Annie; she took it in small bundles in her arms. It pricked and scratched, but she hardly noticed. Back and forth they raced, from the mound of hay in the center to the far sides. No sooner did they get the pile down a little, than another bundle would fall and make it as high as before.

A patter of rain swept the roof, sounding like the feet of hundreds of tiny mice.

"Now it is really raining!" shouted Annie, but Sally paid no attention. The next bundle to come down was a bit damp.

"Are you sure we should spread this?" asked Annie.

"It's only damp on the surface," said Sally. "It will dry out fine here on top of the mow."

"Last one coming up," called Joe.

This bundle felt very wet to Annie. She spread it carefully, as thinly as she could. "I hope it dries out," she prayed silently.

She followed Sally down the steep ladder. Ma and the boys were no longer in the barn. They had gone to the house already. John was giving the cows and calves more hay for the night.

"Where's Joe?" asked Sally.

"That was Barney's team and rack," answered John. "He took it back to the field so they could go home with the hayloader."

It started to pour rain outside.

"We might as well wait here for the last load," said Sally. "No sense running back to the house, only to get wet. Pa and Joe should be here soon."

"But the hay will be soaked," said Annie. "We can't put it on top of that other wet hay."

"Pa will know what to do," said Sally calmly.

Annie crept up the ladder again. She looked carefully to see if the top layer of hay was smoking or steaming. No, it seemed all right. She heard the jingle of the horses' harness and the creak of the whippletree as it turned into the yard next to the barn. She scampered down the ladder as fast as she could and ran to the barn door. Pa and Joe were coming in, soaked to the skin.

"Pa, we're not going to put that wet hay in the barn, are we? I don't want it to go up in smoke."

Pa laughed hard. "It is kind of wet. I guess we can leave it in the rack for now. This shower should pass pretty quick, so the bottom layers will stay dry. Tomorrow, if it's still too wet, we can give that hay to the horses and cows to eat right away. Don't you fret, little worrier; we're not going to let anything happen to our barn."

Annie heaved a sigh of relief. She should have known that Pa would be careful. He always was, and so was Ma. It would take her a long time to learn to be as careful as they were.

The Dangerous Barrel

"John, you won't forget to stop by the store and get me an empty barrel, will you?" asked Ma one morning in August. "The cabbage looks as though it's not going to do so well on account of this dry spell. I want to put up my sauerkraut today, if I can, and the barrel I have been using is rotting to pieces."

"I'll do my best to find one for you," said Pa. He went to the wagon, clicked to the horses, and set off for Dodge.

Annie would have liked to go along, but she knew better than to ask. There was too much to do around the farm these days. Sure enough, as soon as Pa was gone, Ma started giving orders.

"Sally, you and Annie get the two washtubs; scrub and rinse them out good. Then come out to the garden and start bringing in the cabbages as I cut them off. Put them in a pile here on the grass. We can start shredding the cabbage into the washtubs and when your father gets back with the barrel, we'll be ready to start packing down the cabbage."

First the girls carried the two big washtubs out to the pump. They scrubbed the insides with a stiff brush and then rinsed them out carefully several times.

Next, they went to the garden. Ma had already cut most of the heads off the stems, and trimmed away the outer leaves.

"That should do it for now," she said. "We'll leave the others for eating fresh." She walked back to the front yard.

Annie picked up one cabbage, tucked it under her left arm, then lifted up another and balanced it next to the first cabbage. Carefully, she bent down to pick up a third head and that one she tucked under her chin; but when she tried to pick up a fourth cabbage, all of the heads tumbled down.

"Careful! You'll bruise them," said Sally. She was already balancing four cabbage heads in her arms.

"How can you do that?" asked Annie.

"It's not easy, but I think I could manage one more if *you* pile it on top," said Sally.

Annie cautiously placed a fifth large head right in the center of Sally's arms. It did not topple down.

"Why don't you take just three," suggested Sally. "Your arms are much shorter than mine. That way, we can carry eight heads each trip."

Annie picked up three heads, one by one, and they set

off for the front yard where Ma was sitting on a stool next to one of the washtubs. She was wiping the cabbage shredder with a clean, white cloth. Off to one side, Roman and Leo and August were playing with some blocks of wood.

The girls set down the cabbages gently and went for more. Back and forth they trundled, each time loaded down with the heavy green heads. Once, the top head tumbled down from Sally's arms and there was no way she could get it back. Annie had to run and put down her three heads of cabbage before she could help Sally get her load balanced again. It was ten o'clock before they had carried all the cabbages to the pile in the front yard.

Ma had placed the shredder over the larger washtub and was already at work, slicing and shredding the cabbages. The boys looked on with curiosity but did not stand too close.

Whack! With a long butcher knife Ma sliced neatly through a head, right down the middle. She cut away the core in one of the halves, and then put the half-head, cut side down, in the square frame that could slide back and forth over the shredder.

SSS-crunch! SSS-crunch! Each time the cabbage passed over the sharp blade a handful of thin strands would get cut off and drop into the washtub below. Back and forth went Ma's arms in a smooth flow, pressing down and pushing at the same time. As soon as the first half of the cabbage was half sliced away, she plopped the second half into the frame and kept on with her rhythmic pushing and pulling.

"You slice and core them for me," Ma directed Sally. "When my arms get tired we can change off."

"I'll help," offered Annie.

"I wish you could," said Ma, "but it takes a lot of pressure to get the shreds even. I don't think you can press hard enough."

"Let me try," begged Annie.

"I could use a rest," admitted Ma. "Try it for a while and then Sally can take over."

Annie sat down on the bench. Grasping the wooden square on the shredder, she began to move it backwards and forwards.

"Sssss-sssss!" It moved so smoothly Annie could hardly believe it.

"It's easy," she cried.

"Sure it's easy when you just move it back and forth without shredding a thing," said Ma.

Annie moved the square forward again and this time she looked carefully inside the washtub as the cabbage passed over the blade. Only a few tiny wisps of cabbage floated down.

"You must press down hard on the cabbage with one hand, while you push with the other," explained Ma.

Annie tried again, pressing down with all her might; this time a few more strands appeared, but not nearly as many as when Ma did it.

"Let me take over," said Sally. She began to press and push and pull, back and forth, back and forth. Each time a thick flow of cabbage shreds would drop down into the washtub.

"I can't understand what's keeping your father," said Ma as she sliced and cored more cabbages. "He should have been back by now."

"I hear him," cried Annie. Just at that moment the team appeared, coming up the curving hill and into the yard. Pa swung the horses around to the front of the house and called out "Whoa."

"Did you get my barrel, John? I'm ready to start packing the cabbage," called out Ma.

"Well, yes, Anna, I did get a barrel for you, but . . ."

Pa's voice faded away as he lifted the barrel from the back of the wagon and set it down on the grass. Ma walked over to look at it. She lifted the top and staggered backwards.

"Good heavens! John, what were you thinking of? This is a whisky barrel."

"I know, but it's all I could find in Dodge. I went to Mrs. Jereczek's store but she had no empty pickle or cracker barrels. She sent me over to the tavern and this was all they had." Pa looked a little sheepish.

"I don't see how we can use this barrel. Our sauerkraut would be ruined," said Ma.

"I'll give it a good scrubdown for you, first with salt and then with soda. Then we'll let it stand in the sun until it's completely dry. That should do the trick, don't you think?" Annie could see Pa was anxious to please Ma.

"Well, all right. I guess we can wait a day or so. Sally, bring me one of the crock jars from the pantry. We can put up this batch of cabbage we shredded already. And then you and Annie will have to carry the cabbage heads down to the cellar to keep cool."

"Oh, no!" groaned Annie. "Do we have to? Then we'll have to carry them all back again tomorrow or the next day."

"Come on, help load me up," interrupted Sally. She knew that Ma was already annoyed at having to wait for her barrel.

The girls took one load of cabbages off to the root cellar. Then they went to the pantry where Ma had two large crock jars standing empty. Sally lifted one and hoisted it in her arms. It was heavy.

"Open the door for me," she called.

Annie held the door open, shooing away the flies with

her apron, so they would not go into the house. By the water pump at the side of the house she saw Pa bending over the barrel, with one arm inside. The boys had followed him and were standing near, staring at him.

"Whew!" Pa stood up straight. "That's enough to make a fellow dizzy." Pa dipped his brush in a pail of salt water and then leaned over the barrel again. Leo went up close and tried to peer inside. He was curious to see what Pa was doing.

"Don't come so close," warned Pa. "Annie, you take the boys away and watch them. It's dangerous for them around here."

Annie took Leo and August by the hand and Roman followed. They went around to the front yard again.

"Why is it dangerous?" asked Roman.

"I don't know," answered Annie. She wondered what Pa had meant. Could it be that the barrel would explode?

For a while, Annie and the boys watched Ma as she packed the cabbage into the crock jar, sprinkling it with salt on every layer. She pressed each layer down hard, so that the shredded leaves would get juicy.

Annie could not forget what Pa had said. "Why is that barrel dangerous?" she wondered. She did not want Pa to get hurt. She walked to the corner of the house and peeked around it. Now she could see that Pa had tipped the barrel on its side. He was kneeling in front of it, with his head and arms inside. As he scrubbed away, Annie could hear him singing softly. "How can it be dangerous if he is singing?" she asked herself. She turned and walked back to Ma, who was just topping off the crock jar with the last handfuls of cabbage.

"There, that should do it," said Ma as she placed an old dinner plate on top of the cabbage. On top of the plate she placed a smooth, round stone.

"Annie, tell your pa to hurry up with that barrel, and when he's finished, he should take this into the pantry; or better yet, down into the root cellar. Sally, you'd better get some vegetables from the garden and help me start dinner."

Annie ran back to the side of the house where Pa was cleaning the barrel. He was still kneeling down and scrubbing away with his head inside the barrel, only now he was singing loudly and pushing the brush back and forth to the rhythm of the music. It sounded funny and hollow. At first, Annie did not want to interrupt him. She watched and listened for about five minutes.

Swish! Swish! went Pa's brush. His voice started to sound funny and wavery.

"Pa," called Annie loudly, so he could hear. "Ma wants to know if you'll finish soon. You're supposed to carry the crock of sauerkraut down to the cellar."

Pa stopped singing and slowly poked his head out of the barrel. His eyes looked funny. He stared at Annie for a moment, didn't say a word, and then poked his head back into the barrel and continued his scrubbing and singing:

Jeden, dwa, trzy, cztery, pięć;
Pani matko, gdzie jest zięć?
Może tu, może tam;
Piwo z baryłki piję...

One, two, three, four, five and then;
Tell me, mother, where's your son?
Maybe there, maybe here;
Drinking up a barrel of beer . . .

She knew that song, but the words did not go like that.

"Pa, didn't you hear me?" she cried. She was worried that he might be getting sick from that dangerous barrel.

Once more Pa pulled his head out and straightened up.

"Yah, sure I heard. Just wanna finish thish barrel." Back his head went, ducking into the round barrel top.

Annie ran to the house. Ma was in the kitchen, starting to get things ready for dinner.

"Ma, come quick," begged Annie. "I think Pa's sick from that dangerous barrel."

Bang! went the stove lid as Ma dropped it in place and hurried to the door. Over Annie's head she could see her husband, singing inside the barrel as he slowly pushed the brush back and forth.

Jeden, dwa, trzy, cztery, pięć;
Pani matko, gdzie jest zięć?
Może tu, może tam;
Piwo z baryłki piję!

One, two, three, four, five and then;
Tell me, mother, where's your son?
Maybe there, maybe here;
Drinking up a barrel of beer!

"Jesus, Mary and Joseph!" breathed Ma. She always said that, like a prayer, whenever something frightened her. Rushing over to Pa, she pulled him by the feet.

"John, come out of that barrel. You're getting drunk!"

Pa slowly lifted his head out. He was still singing, but then he stopped abruptly.

"'Lo, wifey, thish barrel almos' finish."

He was about to stick his head in again, when Ma cried out, "John, you *are* drunk! Stand up and walk with me. We have to get some clean air into your lungs."

Pa staggered to his feet, but no sooner was he up than

he crumpled down in a heap.

"Good Lord, he can't even stand up," wailed Ma. "Annie, run and get Sally to help me."

Annie tore up to the garden, where Sally and the boys were digging up carrots for dinner.

"Sally, come and help Ma, quick. Pa is sick or drunk or something."

Sally did not even wait to see if the boys could keep up. She ran as fast as she could to the pump. Annie and the boys followed, not far behind.

Pa was singing again. Ma knelt down on one side of him and Sally on the other. They each put one of his arms over their shoulders and then pulled him up. Pa swayed for a moment and seemed ready to topple over again, but they managed to keep him balanced.

"We'll walk around with him a little," said Ma as she tried to take a few steps. With each one, Pa lurched against her, almost pushing her over.

"I think we'd better give him some coffee and put him to bed," said Sally. "It will be easier for him to sleep it off."

Ma nodded her head in agreement. While Annie held the screen door open, they eased him into the house, step by step. As soon as they were in the kitchen, Pa wanted to turn around.

"Gotta finish barrel," he protested.

"The barrel is finished, John, and so are you," said Ma in exasperation. "Come along to the bedroom now and have a nap." Slowly, they eased Pa into the room and down on the bed. His head fell back against the pillow and he closed his eyes. Ma went into the kitchen and came back in a moment with a cup of hot, black coffee. She tried holding it up to Pa's lips, but he could not drink. His head would just slide off to one side.

"He'll be all right, Ma," said Sally. She sounded so sure of herself. Annie looked at her in wonder.

Ma burst into sobs and hurried from the room, then through the kitchen and out the door to the pump. She tipped the barrel right side up and stood over it help-lessly, with the tears streaming down her cheeks. Annie and Sally followed her, silent and thoughtful. Their little brothers stood in the kitchen doorway, behind the screen door, too scared to come out.

"Ma, don't cry," said Sally softly. "It wasn't Pa's fault he got drunk. He was only trying to help you."

Ma said not a word, but continued to cry.

"We can use this barrel as a rain barrel. That will sweeten it up. Tomorrow, Joe can go to Dodge to ask around for another barrel, or maybe some more big crock jars."

Annie could see that Ma was trying to control her tears. Sometimes Ma cried a little bit, but she hadn't cried so hard since last year, when baby Jacob died. Annie was worried. "I wonder if Pa is really sick?" she thought.

At last, Ma's sobbing stopped and she wiped her eyes with her apron. She looked up at Sally and sighed.

"I don't know what I would do without you. Some-times it gets to be just too much for me." Her eyes got shiny again and her face puckered a little. It looked as though she might start crying again, but then she laughed a little.

"He did look silly, didn't he, singing in that barrel." Ma started to laugh a little more and Sally joined in.

"'Drinking up a barrel of beer,'" repeated Ma, shaking her head as she continued to smile and chuckle. "He was *smelling* up a barrel of whisky, that's what he was doing.

Who would have believed the fumes could be so power-
ful? Why, he could hardly stand up!" Then Ma really
started to laugh out loud, remembering how funny Pa
had looked.

Sally laughed, too, and Annie and the boys nervously
joined in. They had been scared, but now that Ma was
laughing instead of crying, everything seemed all right.

Ma sniffed inside the barrel. "It does seem a lot
weaker," she said. "But I think you had a good idea,
Sally. We'd better let it sit full of rain water for a while.
That should soak out the rest of that whisky smell. Let's
roll it over to the corner there, under the eaves, where it
will catch as much rain as possible." They rolled the
barrel into place and stood it up.

"Now you stay away from that barrel, you hear?" Ma
warned Annie and the boys.

"I'll fill it half full of water," said Sally. "That way it
won't tip over before the next rainfall, and it can get a
good start." While Sally carried pail after pail of water
from the pump, Annie and the boys watched. When it
was almost half full, Annie stepped up close to the barrel
and sniffed. A sharp, sour smell crept up her nose.

"Ugh!" she cried. "I'm staying away from there. And
you'd better, too, or I'll tell Ma," she warned her
brothers. Secretly, she vowed to watch them so they
would never get a chance to go near that dangerous
barrel.

Ma Is Worried

Pa slept the rest of that day. He did not get up for dinner or supper.

"Where's Pa?" asked Joe and John when they came in to eat at noon.

"He's lying down," said Ma. "He's not feeling well."

"But we were supposed to start bringing in the second crop of hay this afternoon," exclaimed Joe in surprise. "John and I got it all raked."

"You'll just have to start it by yourselves," said Ma firmly. "Sally can help you."

Joe started to ask a question but Sally gave him a look that told him he'd better keep quiet. They finished the meal in silence and then Joe, John and Sally set out for the hay field.

"Oh, Mother, I'd like to go with them," pleaded Annie. She thought if she said it nicely, in Polish, her mother might let her go.

"No, Anienka, I need you here to watch the little boys. Take them outside to play so you won't wake up Father."

Annie looked cross and unhappy. She did not want to be always taking care of her brothers. They were too little to play the games she liked, and if she did not watch them carefully, they argued and fought over the same stupid sticks of wood.

"I think I will start your school dress today, since I can't put up my sauerkraut," said Ma with a smile. "I will need you here to measure the pieces as I go along."

Annie beamed. Now she was not cross at all. Trying on the pieces for a new dress was much more fun than going haying. Mostly, she had to wear dresses that Sally had worn as a little girl. Ma had packed them away in a trunk and each year she would bring out the ones that fit her. But for her first day of school she was going to have a new dress, made just for her.

For a half-hour or more, Annie played with the boys. Then she took Leo and August in for their naps, while Roman stayed outside to play by himself for a while.

"Come here; let me try this waist on you," said Ma, beckoning to Annie. "I decided to stitch it together right away. It should fit you fine because I made the pieces the same size as Sally's first-grade dress."

Annie slipped her arms through the long sleeves and her head through the round neck. Something did not feel right about it. The sleeves seemed long and floppy and the neck sagged low.

"Oh, no!" cried Ma. "This is way too big for you. How could I have cut it so wrong? Nothing seems to be going

right for me today!" Ma flipped the waist up and over
Annie's head and arms and then flung it on the table; she
burst into tears.

Annie stood in shocked silence. This was the second
time Ma was crying today. Whatever was the matter?

This time Ma stopped crying almost immediately. She
wiped her eyes and picked up the waist.

"Serves me right, I guess. I should have measured
before sewing it up. You always were smaller than Sally,
even as a baby."

Snip, snip! went Ma's scissors at one of the seams.
Rrrrip! She tore it apart from top to bottom. Then she did
the same for all the other seams.

Annie sat quietly, not moving or saying a word. She
could see that Ma was angry about something. As soon as
Ma had measured the pieces against her chest and back
and arms, Annie wanted to slip away quietly. But just
then Joe and Sally and John came into the yard with the
first load of hay.

"I have to go help them unload," said Ma with a sigh. She folded up the material and set it on the sewing machine. "Your dress will have to wait."

While Ma was up at the barn, Annie went to the woodpile.

"Let's bring in the wood now," she said to Roman. He looked up in surprise. He hadn't heard Ma tell Annie to carry in the wood.

"We're going to surprise her," said Annie. They carried in several armloads, filling the woodbox to the top. Then Annie pumped a pail of water and carried it into the kitchen.

When the boys woke up from their naps, she gave them each a piece of jelly bread and took them out to play again. Up by the barn she could see Ma pulling the horses' reins to make them stop. Joe was standing in the rack, holding the trip rope. He jerked it, and Annie knew that inside the barn, a big bundle of hay had dropped down to the haymow, where Sally and John were spreading it out.

"That's the last of it," she heard Joe call out. Ma handed him the reins and came slowly back toward the house. Annie wondered if she would notice the wood and the water. But Ma walked right past and did not say a word. She looked tired as she lowered herself into the rocking chair.

"I think I'll rest for a bit," she said.

Annie stayed outside, playing with the boys; every now and then she peeped inside to see what Ma was doing. Each time she looked she saw Ma sitting in the same position, rocking softly, with her eyes closed. She did not get up or move until Annie called: "They're back with another load of hay."

It was almost four o'clock.

"Feed the chickens and geese," said Ma quietly as she went out the door. Annie was surprised, but she said nothing. Usually, that was Sally's chore, and she only helped her. Now Ma must think she was old enough to do it herself.

"What shall I bring in from the garden for supper?" asked Annie. That was also one of Sally's jobs, but maybe Ma wanted her to do that today, too.

Ma looked at Annie for a few moments. She seemed to have a question in her eyes. Then it was gone.

"Dig up some potatoes. And then bring up one of the cabbage heads from the cellar."

For the rest of the afternoon, Annie was kept busy doing these chores and watching out for her brothers. They ate supper late because it took the boys longer to do the milking without Pa's help. Then they all had to help unload the last rack of hay into the barn, before it got dark. Even Roman helped, spreading the hay with Sally and John and Annie.

When it was all done, they were so tired, they washed up and went right to bed. In the dusky moonlight, Annie could see that Sally was not sleeping.

"Why was Ma crying so much today?" whispered Annie.

Sally hesitated before she answered.

"Because she's worried that the baby is going to die again."

Annie sucked in her breath. She was almost too afraid to ask anything more.

"What baby?" she asked at last. August wasn't a baby any longer, and baby Jacob had died last year. How could he die again?

"The new baby," answered Sally. "Ma's going to have another baby soon and she is worried that it will die, just like baby Jacob."

"So *that's* what Pa meant when he said another one was coming," thought Annie. Now it was all beginning to make sense. It was true. Ma looked the same as she had looked right before baby Jacob was born. If this new baby died soon after being born, like Jacob, would that mean Pa was going to leave the farm?

"Sally, we have to pray for Ma and the new baby," gasped Annie. They had been so tired, they had forgotten to say their prayers.

Quietly, they slid out of bed and knelt down. Sally whispered the first part of each prayer, and Annie answered her, just as they had been taught.

"Oh, please, God, don't let the new baby die," prayed Annie silently, as they crawled back into bed. She shivered and started to cry a little. Sally reached out to put her arms around her sister.

"Don't worry. Everything will come out for the best," she said.

Holding on to each other, they fell asleep.

Hunger Pains

For the next two weeks, Annie carefully watched Ma. She always seemed to be tired; some days she would sit in the rocking chair for hours, resting with her eyes closed. Annie and Sally helped grate and put up all the cabbage in the new sauerkraut barrel Joe had found in Dodge. They helped core and slice dozens of apples and spread them on cloths to dry in the sun.

One day, Ma finished Annie's dress, except for the buttonholes and hem.

"You can do the rest, can't you?" she asked Sally. Annie could see that Sally was pleased. She had never cut and stitched buttonholes by herself, without Ma's help.

71

All afternoon Sally measured carefully, cut cautiously and sewed steadily. By suppertime, Annie's dress was ready. She slipped it on and tried to look at herself in the small mirror above the kitchen sink. The shiny, ruffled collar that stood up around the yoke framed her face and seemed to reflect the red of her hair. It was the nicest dress she had ever had and it made her feel special.

At last it was the first day of school. Sally packed sandwiches for herself and John and Anna. Joe did not go to school anymore. He stayed home to help Pa.

"Take two apples each," said Ma. "And then save one to eat on the way home. You know how hungry you always get."

"I have them, Ma," answered Sally as she pressed down the covers of their tin dinner pails. Then it was time to go. Pine Creek was seven miles away. It would take them a long time to walk there.

"Let's cut across to Prondzinski's," suggested John.

"No, it's better if we take the main road," insisted Sally. "You want to meet up with the others, don't you? We can take the shortcut on the way home."

They had followed the valley road for only a short distance when they heard a call from behind.

"Hey! Wait up for us." Effie and Vic and Damazy came puffing up. They had started out from the neighboring farm just about the same time. Effie was carrying her dinner pail in one hand and a pail of dahlias in the other.

They rounded the curve and there were more children, coming out from the side road. Every quarter mile or so, someone else would join them from one of the farms nestled side by side in the valley. When they reached the end of the valley road, coming down the steep hill were Felix, Alex, Martin and Stance. Now there were more than twenty children, all walking toward Pine Creek.

The girls walked together in a group and a little behind them walked the boys. Sally had many friends to walk with, but Annie had still met no other girls who were starting first grade.

"Aren't there going to be any girls in my class?" she asked Sally as they walked along.

"Don't worry, there are sure to be some," Sally assured her. "Why don't you walk with Florence and Bibiana and Serafina? They are only one grade ahead of you."

Annie looked at the three girls. They were talking excitedly to each other, happy to be back together in second grade. She could see that they did not want any first-grader tagging along.

"I'll just have to walk by myself," sighed Annie. She glanced off to the right and then to the left. Somehow, the road did not look the same as when they drove on it with a wagon or buggy. It was a beautiful day, sunny and hot. The grasshoppers jumped out from the weeds at the side of the road. Every now and then a patch of goldenrod gleamed bright and yellow amid the grassy clumps. The girls would pounce on it and pick the best stems. By the time they approached Pine Creek, they each carried a small bunch of flowers.

They waited in the schoolyard for a few minutes. Then a Sister came out, ringing a handbell. Sally took Annie to the door of the classroom for the first three grades. She peeked inside.

"I think that is a new teacher," she whispered. "I don't know her name." The Sister came to the door. She smiled at them.

"This is my sister Annie," said Sally. "I'm up in seventh grade." Then she hurried away, up the stairs.

"I'm Sister Pelagia. Come in and take a seat in one of the front rows, Annie."

"That's my second name," said Annie, eager to be friendly.

"Fine. But please take your seat now. You must learn to sit up straight and quiet, until the class has assembled."

Annie took a seat in the second row, next to a girl with soft brown curls. She sat up and tried not to move or wiggle. Finally, the last two children came in and took their places.

"Good morning, children," said Sister Pelagia.

The older children in the back rows sprang to their feet. The new first-graders then did the same, looking around fearfully to see if they were doing it right.

"Good morning, Sister," answered the three classes, led by the third-graders.

Annie felt as though she were in a dream. She followed Sister Pelagia's instructions; most of them did not seem to make any sense. Why did they have to keep making ovals on their slates, only to erase them and start all over again? Later they chanted certain sounds in unison, repeating them over and over again after Sister Pelagia, as she pointed to something on the board: ma me mi mo mu. Sister called them syllables. But Annie wanted to learn words. She was not sure she was going to like school. She had to go to the toilet, but she was afraid to ask where it was. Worst of all, she was so hungry she could hardly stand it. At home, Ma always gave them a piece of bread and jelly when they got hungry.

Just when she thought she could bear it no longer and would have to say something, Annie saw Sister Pelagia close the books on her desk and tuck them in the drawer.

Then Sister announced: "It is now time for recess; children, please line up at the door."

At last they could go to the toilet and have a drink. Some of the children took things out of their dinner pails and started to eat, so Annie took out one of her apples and bit into it quickly. It tasted wonderful. She finished it as fast as she could and then walked over to the big field behind the school. Some of her classmates were playing a game of tag, but she was too shy to join in yet.

The rest of the morning was not as bad. Sister explained how you could make words by putting the syllables together.

"I think I'm beginning to catch on," Annie said to herself as she saw the other first-graders continue to repeat syllables. Later, while Sister Pelagia worked with the second grade, the first-graders had to copy the syllables from the blackboard into their copybooks.

"This is easy," thought Annie as she wrote over and over again, one below the other:

ma	me	mi	mo	mu
ma	me	mi	mo	mu
ma	me	mi	mo	mu

The moment the clock showed both hands straight up, the bell rang and all the children reached for their dinner pails.

"Today you may eat outside in the schoolyard," said Sister. "When the weather is not so nice you will have to stay inside and eat."

Annie searched for Sally, and went to sit near her.

"Don't you want to sit with the first-grade girls?" asked Sally.

Annie blushed and shook her head. She was still too shy to talk to them on her own. Besides, she noticed that most of them had gone to eat with their older sisters. They ate their thick slices of bread and butter, filled with slabs of meat. Sally bit into one of her apples. Annie reached into her pail to take out her second apple. Then she hesitated. "Ma said we should save one for on the way home," she thought. She brought her hand out empty.

"Aren't you going to have one of your apples?" Sally asked in surprise. Annie did not want to admit that she had eaten one of them already.

"I guess I'll have it after all. I wasn't sure I was hungry for it now." Annie slid her hand into the pail again, took the apple out, and closed the cover fast, before Sally could glance in. Now she had nothing more to eat.

"I hope I don't get hungry on the way home," thought Annie.

All afternoon, Annie thought about food.

"I am not hungry," she said to herself over and over. All around her, it seemed that everyone was talking about food.

"The cow gives milk," read one of the second-graders aloud. "Every day the farmer milks the cow in the morning and in the evening."

"Oh, how I would like to have a tall, cool glass of milk," thought Annie.

"Look what I saved for afternoon recess," said one of the second-graders as he held up two pieces of candy. His father owned a store in Dodge. He could probably have candy every day.

"Oh, if only I could have one of those pieces of candy," thought Annie. She only got candy at Christmas and Easter. But the boy did not offer a piece to her.

"Give us this day our daily bread," intoned the two classes as they recited their prayers at the end of the school day.

"If only I had some of my bread left to eat," thought Annie.

Whooping and shouting and laughing, the children set off for home. Once again, Sally and the older girls took the lead. Annie trailed behind them, and the boys followed still farther back. This time they took shortcuts across some fields, but it was still a long way.

Annie's stomach began to growl. She walked slower and slower, falling behind Sally. Florence walked almost as slowly as she did. John and the neighbor boys were even farther behind, dawdling along and fooling around with each other.

Sally and the girls came to the Kulas farm. "We'll cut across here," she called back to Annie. "Can you find your way all right?"

"Yes," Annie shouted back.

Sally hesitated. "John, walk with Annie and Florence," she called.

Annie and Florence waited for a moment to let John catch up with them. He and Vic and Damazy were tramping along together. They all left the road and started across the field.

"Gee, I'm hungry," said Vic.

"Me, too," said John. "Annie, do you have anything left in your pail?"

In answer, Annie shook her head. "Gurgle, gurgle, gurgle," went her stomach.

"You're hungry, too, huh?"

Annie nodded her head. She was so hungry she wanted to cry.

"Are you really, really hungry?" asked John. "So

hungry you might starve?"

Once more Annie nodded her head.

"I'm hungry, too," cried Florence.

John looked off to the right with a gleam in his eyes.

"That's the field where the Kulases grow their rutabagas. Mrs. Kulas wouldn't want you girls to starve, so I'm sure she won't mind if we dig up a couple of rutabagas."

John was running across the field before anyone could reply. Vic and Damazy ran after him. Soon they were back, each carrying a round, yellow-and-purple rutabaga. John took out his pocketknife and began to peel away the thick skin. He sliced off a crisp, yellow chunk of rutabaga and handed it to Annie.

"Are you sure it's all right to eat it?" she asked.

"All I know is, Mrs. Kulas wouldn't want little girls to starve," answered John.

Quickly, Annie snatched the rutabaga slice and began to chew it. It tasted so good and crunchy and juicy that she could hardly wait for John to slice more. He gave everyone a piece and then another piece.

They walked along, munching on rutabaga. Before long, they passed the Prondzinskis' and Florence left them. Two more fields, across the creek bed, and they were on the valley road again.

John began slicing the last rutabaga. He gave one last chunk to Vic and one to Damazy and then they separated.

"Hurry up! We have to finish this before we get home," urged John.

Annie did not want any more rutabaga. Now she was full—so full, her stomach hurt.

"Ma says it's a sin to throw away food, so I guess I have to eat it," thought Annie. Somehow, she knew that she did not want to take any of the rutabaga home. She chewed and chewed, forcing herself to swallow the last bites.

As they entered the house, Ma was just starting out the door. "I was getting a little worried about you," she said. "I almost sent Sally back to see what happened to you. She said you were right behind her. Did you have a nice first day at school?"

Ma's soft, gentle voice was worried, but not scolding.

"Oh, Ma," cried Annie, unable to hold back her tears. "I got so hungry during the day, all I could think about was food. I didn't save an apple for after school, like you told us to, and I was starving on the way home. John said

I shouldn't starve so he went and got some rutabagas from the Kulases' field and . . ." Annie's voice trailed off in sobs. The big, painful knot in her stomach grew bigger.

John was about to go out the door when Ma stopped him.

"Did you stop and ask Mrs. Kulas if you could have the rutabagas?"

"No, Ma." John hung his head as he answered.

"John, how could you steal like that?" asked Ma sadly.

"Well, Annie said she was so hungry she was going to starve and . . ." John's voice trailed off when he looked at Ma. He could see that she was disappointed and angry.

"Well, I'm afraid you'll not get any supper, either of you, until you dig up some rutabagas from our garden and take them right now to Mrs. Kulas. You have to tell her how sorry you are. It will probably be dark by the time you get back, but you know the way, John. Take a lantern, so you can see on the way home."

Without another word, John went to get three rutabagas, and he and Annie set off. She could hardly tell where she was walking, she was crying so hard. How could Ma make her do something like this? Now she would always be ashamed to look at Mrs. Kulas. They walked the entire distance without saying a word. By the time they reached the Kulases' front yard, Annie had stopped crying.

"What am I going to say?" wondered Annie.

They did not have to knock on the screen door. Mrs. Kulas was standing right outside it, watching them approach. She must have seen their lantern.

"Children, what's the matter? Has your mother taken sick or something?" Mrs. Kulas did not even seem to notice the rutabagas in their hands.

"Well," said John, "it's like this. On our way home from school we got hungry and, well . . ." John stammered and hesitated.

"We were starving," interrupted Annie. "We couldn't stand it so John said you would not want us to starve and he picked some rutabagas from your field, only Ma said that's stealing and she sent us back here. We didn't mean to steal, Mrs. Kulas," cried Annie, and she burst into tears again.

Mrs. Kulas looked at John. "Your Ma was right. That is stealing. But you're not the only children who make a secret stop in our rutabaga patch. Last year I hardly got enough to keep for winter." She shook her head sadly.

"We won't do it again, we promise," said John.

Mrs. Kulas smiled. "Better not make a promise you can't keep. How would it be if I tell you that you can pick one rutabaga whenever you get really hungry on the way home? Not every day, mind you! Just every now and then, when you think you can't make it home without a bite of something."

"Gee, thanks, Mrs. Kulas," said John.

Annie just looked up at her gratefully. They handed Mrs. Kulas the rutabagas and set off for home again. Annie felt like running, she was so happy and relieved. The knot in her stomach was disappearing. In fact, she was starting to get hungry again.

"But I'll never eat another rutabaga from the Kulases' field," she promised out loud.

"Didn't you hear what Mrs. Kulas said?" asked John. "Never make a promise you can't keep."

"I'll keep it," said Annie, determinedly. She knew that every day after this, she would be sure to save something from her dinner pail, no matter how hungry she was at noon, so she would always have something to eat on the way home. Besides, just knowing that the rutabagas were in the Kulases' field would help, especially since Mrs. Kulas had said they could have one now and then.

"That's it," said Annie to herself. "It's when I know there's nothing to eat that I think I'm hungry. If I know there always is something, then I won't think about eating so much. No, I'm sure of it. I will never eat another rutabaga from the Kulases' field."

Matthew

For the next few weeks, Annie lived up to her promise.
Not once did she let John take a rutabaga from the
Kulases' field. Sometimes she saved enough bread and
butter to share with him, so that he could have something
to eat on the way home, too.

One Monday morning in late September, Annie got
dressed as usual and went to the kitchen. Sally was
stirring a pot of oatmeal. She was wearing her everyday
dress, not the one she wore to school.

"Are you going to school like that?" asked Annie.

"I'm not going today," answered Sally.

"Why not?"

"Ma's not feeling well. I have to stay home and help her."

"Does that mean the baby's coming?" asked Annie eagerly. "I want to stay home and watch the baby come."

"Oh, Annie, you can't do that," laughed Sally. "Besides, I'm not sure it is coming today. Joe went to get Near Grandmother. She will know what to do. But Ma says you should go to school with John. You won't be scared, will you?"

"No, I won't be scared. But I want to stay here with you."

"You can't. Ma said so, and that's final." Sally's voice was firm.

While eating her oatmeal, Annie was thinking. She was wondering how the new baby would come. When Jacob had come, she had not known about it ahead of time. She woke up one morning and there he was. Vaguely, she remembered it had been the same with Leo and August. This was the first time she knew in advance that a baby was coming and she wanted to see how it got there.

"Here are your dinner pails," said Sally. "Call John from the barn and tell him it's time to wash up and go."

With a sigh, Annie went to get John. Ten minutes later they were on their way.

"You be sure to walk close to Annie," Sally called to John in warning. "And hurry home after school."

The road seemed longer than usual. Once they got to school, Annie forgot about not being there for the baby's arrival. She liked school now, especially reading and writing lessons. It was fun to put the syllables together to make words. When Sister Pelagia called on her for arithmetic sums, she always knew the answer. Never, not once, had she been smacked on the knuckles because of fooling around or not paying attention.

After school she and John walked home together, taking as many shortcuts as they could. They did not wait for any of the other children. They ran the last half-mile, anxious to find out about the baby.

Sally was standing at the woodpile in the yard, loading up her arms with sticks of firewood. The younger boys were there, too, helping as best they could by carrying one or two sticks.

"Did the baby come?" yelled Annie from across the yard, as soon as she saw Sally. Sally did not answer.

"Did the baby come?" repeated Annie, coming closer to the woodpile.

"Yes," answered Sally, but she was not smiling. "The baby came but he is very sickly, and so is Ma. Try to be real quiet when you go inside. Don't go yelling like that. Ma and the baby need rest."

"Are they going to die?" asked Annie fearfully.

"Let's hope and pray they won't," said Sally. "Come and help carry in wood, and then feed the chickens and geese so I can start supper. And gather any eggs I might have missed this morning."

Annie put her dinner pail down by the door and went to fill her arms with a load of wood. She followed Sally and the boys into the house. Carefully, they unloaded the wood, stick by stick, into the woodbox, trying not to make any noise. Even the little boys were careful not to drop any sticks.

Annie took off her school dress and put on her old, everyday working clothes.

"Come on," she whispered to Roman and Leo. "You can help me scatter the chicken feed." They went out to do their chores.

When they were finished, Annie was about to go in the house but Sally stopped her at the door, holding out a tin pitcher.

"Bring me some more milk from the barn; I want to make a custard for Ma."

Annie ran to the barn where Pa and Joe were still milking. Pa was leaning his head against the side of Brownie. His fingers stripped the milk down in long, slow glides. He had such a frown on his face, she was almost afraid to speak to him.

"Pa," she said at last, "Sally wants more milk to make a custard for Ma."

Without a word, Pa swung his milk pail out and filled the pitcher almost full. Then he went back to his steady stripping.

That evening, they ate supper quietly. There was none of the joking or laughing like on other days. Pa didn't tease Annie as he often had the last two weeks, by asking her: "Did you get your knuckles rapped today in school?"

Grandmother spooned some food into a dish. She was going to take it home to Grandfather.

"I'll be back first thing in the morning," she said.

"Joe, hitch up the team and take your grandmother home," said Pa.

"I can walk," protested Grandmother. But Annie could see she looked tired. Joe had already gone outside, without a word of complaint at the extra work.

"I'll ride with Joe and Grandmother," offered Annie.

"Don't you have any lessons to write out?" asked Pa.

"No, Father. I did them all in school." Pa nodded his head then. She could go.

Annie sat between Joe and Grandmother on the wagon seat. It would take them only about ten minutes to get to

Near Grandfather's farm. The road was dim and winding, but the horses knew the way. They turned off the valley road onto the narrower road leading to the farm.

"Grandmother," whispered Annie. "Mother won't die, will she?"

"No, child; your mother is weak but she will be fine after she gets her strength back. But the little baby . . ." Here Grandmother hesitated, with a question in her voice. "My heart goes out to your mother. I know what it is to lose babies. I was left with only your father."

Annie thought about that for a moment. It was true she had no aunts and uncles from Pa's side. But what did Grandmother mean? Was she scared that Ma would end up with only one child?

"Grandmother, you don't think we're all going to die and leave Ma with only one?" Annie was worried which one it would be.

"Well, child, we all have to die some day, but you and Sally and Joe and the little boys are growing up fine. You don't have to think about that for a long time—not until you are an old grandmother, like me."

"Grandmother, you can't die; you have to help Mother," pleaded Annie.

Grandmother put her arm around Annie and gave a soft smile.

"I hope the good Lord does give me a few more years," she said. "But we all have to be ready when our time comes. For some of us it's when we are old and gray and for others it's like your new baby brother—the Lord wants them right away. When you are a big girl, you will be able to understand it better. In the meantime, you must be good and help your mother as much as you can."

They pulled up in front of the house and Grandmother got out.

"Goodnight," she called. "Go with God."

Joe had been silent all the way. He turned the wagon around and they began the ride home. They did not speak at all. The lantern that hung at the side of the wagon cast a soft glow on the dried weeds and grasses as it passed by. Except for the little pool of lantern light that moved with them, all was filled with the deep dusk of early night.

Back in their own yard, Annie jumped down and ran to the house while Joe went to unhitch the team and bed them down for the night. Pa was sitting at the kitchen table with Sally and John. The little boys were already in bed. In front of Pa was the big Polish *Book of the Saints*.

"Today is the Feast of St. Matthew," he said. "Your new brother will be named Matthew." Then he began to read aloud from the book. It told all about how St. Matthew was not liked because he was a tax collector. But Jesus loved him all the same and even went to a farewell dinner that Matthew gave for all his friends, who were considered sinners and outcasts just as he was. Later, after Pentecost, Matthew went preaching in Syria and Arabia and many other places. He was not afraid, even when people threw stones at him.

"St. Matthew was such a strong man," thought Annie. "Maybe he will help baby Matthew." When she and Sally said their prayers that night, they added a prayer to St. Matthew.

The next morning, Annie awoke at her usual time and hurried down to the kitchen. This morning, Sally had on her best dress.

"Are you going to wear that to school?" asked Annie.

"I'm going to church, not to school. We are taking Matthew to be baptized. You won't have to walk today. You can ride along."

"Is Pa going?" asked Annie.

"Yes, he will drive our wagon and Grandmother and Grandfather will follow in their cart. They are going to be godparents. I'll come back with them so Pa can get the doctor, to see if there is anything he can do."

"Oh, Sally, you're missing another day of school," cried Annie.

"I'll probably have to miss a lot more," said Sally matter-of-factly. "It can't be helped. Someone has to stay and help Ma."

Annie felt guilty. Now that she liked school so much she did not want to stay home. Yet she knew she should offer to help.

"I'll stay home if you want me to," she blurted out at last.

"There's no need to; I can manage. It's better if you don't miss too many days in first grade."

Sally finished fixing the dinner pails and then carefully wrapped up the baby in blankets. Only his tiny face was showing. He did not cry at all and hardly moved or wiggled.

"Will he cry when the priest pours water?" wondered Annie. She wanted him to cry hard to show he was strong and well, but at the same time she did not want him to scream, as she had when she was baptized. She wanted to be the only one Pa joked about. She would have liked to ask Pa to tell her the story again, but he was too sad and worried looking.

Pa and Sally sat on the front buggy seat and Annie and Joe sat on the back one. It felt so strange to be riding to school. Grandmother and Grandfather followed right behind them in their two-wheeled cart. They passed Effie and her brothers, who stared up at them. Annie thought Pa might offer them a ride but he went right past as though he had not seen them.

They arrived in Pine Creek early. School would not start for more than a half-hour yet. While Pa went to get the priest, Annie and the others filed into church. They sat in a back pew, waiting near the baptismal font.

Soon Father Gara came with Pa and prepared everything for the baptism. He poured some of the holy water into a small metal pitcher and held it over a candle, warming it.

Baby Matthew did not cry out when the water was poured over his head. He only whimpered softly.

"Oh, I do wish he would scream," prayed Annie. "I won't mind at all if Pa jokes about him, too." But the baptism ended and little Matthew was quiet and unmoving.

"Wait right outside the school door," Sally told John and Annie. "The others will get here soon. We have to hurry home."

All day Annie thought about Matthew. Maybe the doctor would be able to give him some medicine to make him strong. But when she arrived home that evening, she could see that Sally looked more serious than ever.

"Was the doctor here?" asked Annie. "Did he do something?"

"Yes, he was here," nodded Sally. "But he says there is not much he can do. Little Matthew has very weak lungs. If he can hold his own for a few weeks, he might pull through. But he seems to be getting weaker every moment, not stronger." Sally looked as though she wanted to cry.

Annie didn't know what to say. Sally was so grown up and she always seemed so sure of herself. They did their chores in silence.

Every day after that, Annie and John rushed home from school and every day they sought out Sally first of all, looking at her with questioning eyes. She always shook her head and turned away. Then, one day, two weeks after Matthew had been born, Annie and John came home to find that he had died during the afternoon.

Sally's eyes were red from crying, but Ma did not look as though she had cried at all. She just sat there in the rocking chair, dazed and unmoving. Pa had gone to town to get a small casket and when he came back it was after supper. Ma and Sally washed little Matthew's body and dressed it in a long white dress. They placed it in the soft white folds of the silky cloth lining the casket, and then Pa led them in prayers.

"Now go to bed," he said quietly.

The next day, after Mass in church, they buried Matthew in the cemetery at the top of the hill, next to baby Jacob and baby Francis, who had died before Annie was born. Now Ma was crying, in deep, shuddering sobs. She kept it up all through the final prayers. When Father Gara said the last blessing, he called Matthew an angel in heaven.

"Baby Matthew will like that," thought Annie, as she pictured him flying through the clouds.

They moved away from the grave and Annie went close to her mother, taking her arm.

"Don't cry, Ma. You still have all of us. We're not going to die. Grandmother says so," Annie assured her. But that only made Ma cry harder.

"Hush, Annie," said Pa gently. "No matter how many children she has, it's hard for your mother to lose a baby."

So they were all quiet on the way home, as Ma cried herself out.

A Visit to the City

It took a long time for Ma to gain back her strength. Sally had to stay home and do the cooking, baking and washing, as well as her other chores. Annie felt she should stay home to help, too, but Ma and Sally would not hear of it.

"First grade is important," insisted Sally. "That's when you learn to write and read and do arithmetic. It's hard to catch up if you miss a lot." Annie knew that was true because some of the children in her classroom who were supposed to be in second grade were still doing first-grade work. They had missed a lot of school during their first year, and then over the long summer they had forgotten everything. Sometimes Sister Pelagia got angry with them.

"I don't want to get behind," said Annie.

"Then go to school like a good girl," said Ma, "and do your lessons every day. I only wish I didn't have to keep Sally home."

"Don't worry, Ma," said Sally. "If I can't keep up, I don't mind repeating seventh grade."

Every week Ma got a little stronger, but there was still so much to do, Sally continued to stay home. In the first week of December, Ma wanted to butcher the geese so she could take them to town to sell. She and Sally worked hard, stripping them of their feathers and taking out their innards. Ma had to rest a lot in between, but by Thursday evening they were ready. The geese had frozen stiff and solid during the sharp December nights.

"John, I think we should go to Winona this Saturday to sell the geese," said Ma. "I want to see Mother and Father and buy some things before the winter storms come and we can't get to town."

"I'm willing," said Pa, "as long as the weather holds."

Annie waited expectantly. She was hoping Ma would say she could go along. Sally also looked up eagerly.

"Sally, I am sorry but I think you had better stay here and keep an eye on things with Joe and John. Annie and the little boys can come along."

Sally's eyes showed her disappointment. She had been working so hard it did not seem fair that she must stay behind.

"Do you think we can arrange for Sally to go on the train, right after Christmas, for a visit to Grandfather and Grandmother?" asked Ma, looking at Pa with a smile. Pa nodded.

Sally gasped and laughed in surprise and joy. She could not say a thing. Annie felt a tiny kernel of jealousy explode in her insides, like a popcorn seed. She had never been on a train, and wanted so much to take a ride on one. But Sally had been staying home from school and working all those weeks. She was the one who should get such a nice treat. Still, Annie had to swallow hard to make the jealous feeling go away.

"Annie, here's a quarter. Tomorrow when you're in Winona, I want you to buy a Christmas present for Ma," whispered Sally on Friday evening as they were getting ready for bed.

"What shall I buy?" asked Annie. She had never spent a quarter on anything before, not in her whole life.

"Buy anything you see that you think she might like," said Sally. "I'm sure you'll come across something."

Very early the next morning, they packed the frozen geese carefully under the back seat of the buggy. Pa hitched Lady and Lucky, their best team, to the front, and then the family climbed up and sat down on the seats. Ma was all bundled up in her shawl and lap robe. Pa had placed a cushion of feed sacks and an old blanket on the front seat, so she would not get tired from sitting on the hard wood. It took more than an hour to get to the high wagon bridge that crossed the Mississippi River over to the Minnesota side.

"I hope we don't meet up with any automobiles on the bridge," said Pa as he stopped the horses and stood up to look ahead. "I'm not sure I could handle them."

Seeing nothing ahead, he gave the horses a flick of the reins and they began the uphill climb over the curve of the bridge. Annie shivered with excitement. Each time she looked down over the side of the buggy, she could see the swirling water far below, straight down from the edge of the bridge. It gave her such a funny feeling; she didn't want to look again, but somehow she had to. When she looked up she could see the tall buildings of Winona.

Over on the left was the dome of St. Stanislaus Church. She knew that was near the house where Grandfather and Grandmother lived. The dome was even higher than the tall steeple of their church in Pine Creek. It gleamed and sparkled in the December sun.

When they came to the highest point on the bridge, Pa stopped to pay the toll of twenty-five cents. Then they started the downward curving ride. Now, Annie looked to the right where there were other tall buildings, so many that she could never count them, even though she tried to do it each time they crossed the bridge. The ride was always too short.

"Are we going straight to Grandfather's house?" asked Annie as Pa turned off the bridge.

"No, first we'll stop at Libera's store and see if he wants to buy the geese. And then your mother will certainly want to make a stop at Mrs. Cierzan's." Pa looked at Ma to see if he had guessed right. She smiled and nodded her head.

"I'll take all the geese you have there," said Mr. Libera when they got to his store. "Folks around here still like their goose for Christmas." Pa and Ma talked for a while and then bought some of the things they could not get in Dodge. Then Mr. Libera took a wad of bills and some coins and counted out the money he still owed Ma for the geese.

"Here, Annie," said Ma, and she dropped five pennies into her hand. "That's your spending money."

Annie had been looking carefully, to see if there was something she could buy for Ma with Sally's quarter. Now she had her own five cents. The trouble was, everything she saw at Libera's looked so good, especially the candies. But Pa was already hurrying them out to the buggy. She would have to spend her money elsewhere.

Next they stopped at Mrs. Cierzan's dry goods store. Ma selected yards and yards of fabric of different kinds. During the long winter months she would sew under-clothes, shirts, dresses and aprons for anyone in the family who needed them. Annie looked to see if Ma had her eye on one special piece of goods. She seemed to be buying only things they needed for everyday wear.

"Annie, run outside and tell your Pa I won't be long now," said Ma.

"I'll never get to spend the quarter and my five cents," thought Annie. She went outside where Pa and the boys were waiting in the buggy. They had seen an automobile go by.

"I think that was a Model T," said Pa. "I'd like a closer look at one of those."

"Ma will be ready soon," said Annie. She wondered why she had had to come out to tell Pa that. He did not seem to be fidgeting or thinking Ma was taking a lot of time. They waited and in a few more minutes Ma came out, carrying her bundles.

It was only a short distance to Grandfather's house. When he heard their footsteps on the front porch, he came to the door and exclaimed in surprise: "Well, look who's here!"

They entered the house and Ma, Pa, Annie and the boys all said, *"Niech będzie pochwalony Jezus Chrystus!"*

"Na wieki wiekow, amen!" answered Grandfather.

Then Grandmother threw her arms around Ma, and they both cried a little. They had not seen each other since before baby Matthew was born. Grandmother consoled Ma and whispered something to her. Then she bustled out to the kitchen.

"I wish you folks had given us warning. I could have made something special for dinner. Come, Martha, we'll have to scrape a few things together," said Grandmother.

Aunt Martha was one of Ma's younger sisters. She lived with Grandfather and Grandmother and Uncle Joe, Ma's youngest brother. Aunt Pauline, Ma's youngest sister, lived there part of the time, but just now she was working as a dressmaker in Minneapolis. Annie always found it strange that Uncle Joe was only two years older than her brother Joe.

"Joe, why don't you take the children for a walk while we get dinner," suggested Grandmother. Annie and the boys were glad to hear that. They were tired of sitting such a long time in the buggy. They bundled up again in their warm clothes and scarves and mittens.

"Shall we walk down by the river?" asked Uncle Joe. The boys yelled "Yes" and jumped up and down in excitement. Annie only nodded. She was too shy to say anything.

They walked down to Front Street and there was the levee, edged with a thin strip of ice on the river, for a few feet out. Beyond that, the dark, muddy water rushed and swirled, whipped up in little waves. This was the same water Annie had seen from the top of the bridge, but somehow it looked different. From the bridge, the water had seemed deep blue and mysterious. Here, it looked like plain, brown, ordinary creek water, except that it stretched much farther and wider than any creek she had ever seen.

"It will freeze straight across, pretty soon," said Joe.
Annie did not answer.

"We'll walk up to the steamboat landing and back,"
said Uncle Joe. Along the levee they tramped. Leo and
Roman and August kept running down to skate on the
thin edge of ice, so Annie grabbed hold of Leo's hand and
Joe took August's hand on one side and Roman's on the
other. They walked up to the pier and stared at the big
boat resting in the water. It had a giant paddle wheel and
was much taller and bigger than a house.

"This will probably be the last steamboat for the year,"
said Uncle Joe. "It's leaving tomorrow for the South. The
river's freezing over so fast, it will be lucky to get
through.

Annie did not know what to say to Uncle Joe. He was
talking to her as though she were grown up. They walked
back to the house and then it was time to eat dinner.

At the dinner table, Grandfather talked about life in
Winona. He had sold his farm and moved to town almost
five years ago.

"It's getting better all the time," said Grandfather.
"There is pretty steady work now. You just might want to
try it some day, John."

Annie could see Ma and Pa exchange a quick glance.

"Only thing is," said Pa, "a fellow has to give up a lot
of freedom living in town. I like being my own boss."

Annie breathed a sigh of relief. It sounded as though
Pa was definitely going to stay on the farm. They finished
dinner and stayed for a while longer, but then Pa
announced it was time to go.

"I've still got to stop and get some supplies at the
hardware store, and we want to get back before dark."

Quickly Annie dressed up warmly again and helped Leo and August into their coats. They said "Goodbye" to Grandmother and Aunt Martha and then went out to watch Pa and Grandfather and Uncle Joe get the horses and buggy backed out of the stable. At last they were ready to go, except for Ma. She was still inside, talking with Grandmother. Uncle Joe ran in to get her.

"You might think about what I was saying," said Grandfather to Pa. "It's mighty hard on Anna out there in the valley. I'm sure I could find you work here in Winona."

"I'll think about it," agreed Pa, and just then Ma came out and he and Grandfather stopped talking. Annie wasn't positive she had caught the whole meaning, but it seemed as though Pa was still not sure about staying on the farm.

Pa turned the buggy toward the center of town and drove off. As they got nearer to the big stores, two automobiles passed them, chugging along with a loud noise. Pa stopped in front of R. D. Cone's Hardware and there, on the opposite side of the street, was a big black automobile, surrounded by a group of admirers.

"That's it," cried Pa excitedly. "That's the Model T. Isn't she a beauty, Anna? How would you like to see yourself riding to town in one of those?"

"I would be too scared to ride, that's what," said Ma with a laugh. "I think I'd rather stay with Lady and Lucky."

Pa had a good, long look at the Model T before they went into the hardware store. "I wouldn't be afraid to ride in it," thought Annie. "At least, not if Pa was with me."

While Pa bought some nuts and bolts and nails and

screws of many sizes, Annie looked around at the other things. She saw some pans for the kitchen that Ma might like, but she wasn't sure how much they cost. "Besides," she thought, "I don't think Sally would like this kind of present for Ma. She will have to buy a present in Dodge. And I can spend my five cents there, too."

It was three o'clock before Pa finished and they set off for home. There were quite a few automobiles on the busy streets. Pa took narrow side streets every now and then, so the horses would not get frightened by all the movement. People hurried to and fro, busy with their Saturday errands. It was rather exciting and Annie began to think it might not be so bad to live in the city. But it was scary, too. There were so many strange people and she was always shy and frightened of strangers.

They crossed the high wagon bridge and Annie took one last backward look at Winona. It was fun to visit the city but she was glad they were on their way back home. No matter what Grandfather said, she did not want to live there.

A chill wind came sweeping off the river.

"Brrr!" said Ma, shivering in her seat. She pulled her soft, woolen shawl more tightly around her head and shoulders.

"You need a scarf around your neck to hold that down," said Pa. "Here, take mine." He unwound it from around his ears and neck.

"I couldn't, John. You'll catch cold," said Ma.

"Not any sooner than you. I'll put my collar up and pull my cap down and that should take care of my ears," laughed Pa.

Annie watched Ma bundle herself up well with Pa's scarf. It gave her an idea.

"I can't wait to get home to tell Sally," she thought. "I know just what we can give Ma for Christmas."

Crochet for Christmas

That evening, as soon as they were in bed, Annie told Sally about her plan.

"Ma needs a scarf to wrap around over her shawl. I want you to help me make one. Then we don't have to use your quarter."

"I don't think there's enough time. Tomorrow is already December sixth," whispered Sally.

"It won't take long to crochet a scarf if you help me," insisted Annie.

"But we don't have enough yarn. Grandmother hasn't finished spinning this year's wool. She has been too busy helping Ma."

"Then I'll go and help her," said Annie with finality. She was determined to make the scarf for Ma.

The next day was Sunday and Annie wanted to ride back from church with Grandmother and Grandfather.

"Mother, may I?" she asked politely.

Mother nodded and smiled.

Annie started questioning Grandmother as soon as they were in the cart.

"Did you start spinning this year's wool, Grandmother?"

"Yes, I've just started."

"Do you have a lot of yarn?"

"Pretty much. I still have some from last year."

"Are you going to need it all?"

"Such a question box you are! I don't know how much I need. I will probably give some to your mother."

"May Sally and I have some to crochet a long scarf for Mother?" pleaded Annie.

"So *that's* what all these questions were leading to!" laughed Grandmother. "If I give you the balls of yarn I have ready, then you must come and help me on a few Saturdays. There is still a lot of carding and spinning to do before all the wool is finished."

"I'll come next Saturday, if Mother will let me," promised Annie.

They rode along without talking much after that. Annie was imagining the pretty scarf she and Sally would make for Ma. Soon they came to the road leading to her house. Grandfather stopped the horses.

"No, I'm going with you all the way," insisted Annie. "I want to get the yarn and bring it back so Sally and I can start crocheting today."

"You *are* a little schemer," chuckled Grandfather. He

waited for a few minutes until the other buggy came up close behind them. "Annie's going on with us," he called out. "We'll send her home right after dinner."

First Grandmother and Grandfather had to eat breakfast. They had been fasting so they could go to Communion. Then there were the morning chores to do. Then it was time to start dinner. Annie helped as much as she could but all the while she was thinking: "If only I could take the yarn and run home."

Finally, dinner was over and Annie had dried all the dishes for Grandmother.

"Now, how about a nice nap?" asked Grandfather.

Annie looked at him in dismay. Didn't he know that she had not been taking naps for years and years?

"He's only teasing," Grandmother assured her. "Come, we'll have a look at the yarn."

"You may not like the idea of a snooze, but I do," said Grandfather. He went off to the bedroom, yawning and loosening his shirt buttons.

Grandmother opened a cupboard that stood next to the spinning wheel in one corner of the kitchen. There were several dozen balls of yarn, some a deep, rich red and others in dark blue.

"I'll take the red," blurted out Annie, without even thinking.

Grandmother nodded. "It is a pretty color, isn't it. But I think your mother would prefer the blue."

Annie looked at the bright red and the dull blue. She liked the red so much more and she was sure Ma would, too.

"Here, let me show you something," said Grandmother. "Feel this red ball, and then feel this blue one."

Annie rubbed her hands first over the red one and then

over the blue one. She looked up in surprise.

"The blue one feels nicer, doesn't it?" said Grandmother. "That's because I made it from last year's lambs' wool. This year we had only ewes to shear; I made the red wool from their fleece and it's not as soft. Now, don't you think your mother would like the blue better?"

"Oh, yes," nodded Annie. She wished she could still have the red color, but once she had touched that fluffy, blue yarn, the red seemed scratchy and itchy. She was glad Grandmother had made her feel the difference.

"Let's see; for a good, long scarf you will need about five balls." Grandmother selected the ones that looked best to her and put them on a pile on the kitchen table. Then she got out an old cloth, tied the yarn balls inside, making a neat bundle, and handed it to Annie.

"Are you sure you can carry it all the way home?"

"Yes, I'm sure." Annie nodded. She ran to get her coat and shawl and overshoes. She was anxious to hurry home. Ma always lay down to rest after dinner and Annie wanted to slip inside the house without being seen.

"Goodbye, Grandmother. Thank you for the yarn. I'll come to help you next Saturday," said Annie as she hurried out the door.

She ran almost all the way home. Luckily, Ma was still resting, so Annie could sneak up to the bedroom she shared with Sally, carrying the bundle of yarn. It was cold and frosty upstairs. Not much heat came up through the register over the stove.

"Help me start it off," Annie appealed to Sally. She could crochet if someone did the first few rows for her.

"Right now?"

"Yes, right now! If we want the scarf to be finished by Christmas, without Ma seeing it, we have to work whenever she is lying down," argued Annie.

Wearing their shawls around their shoulders they set to work. First, Sally made a slip knot and then she chain-stitched a long row.

"This is wide enough, isn't it?" Sally held up the row of stitched yarn. Annie nodded. It looked very wide to her. How would they ever get it done?

Sally started to add on rows. In and out went the crochet hook, first up one row, then down the next.

"Now you try it," said Sally.

Annie poked the crochet hook through the two loops, twisted the yarn over and then pulled the hook and the yarn through the loopholes. She went up almost one entire row before Sally stopped her.

"That's not tight enough. See how it's puckering here? You have to get it just right—tight but not too tight." She pulled out the row of stitches and Annie had to start over again. For an hour they kept at it, pushing the crochet hook in and out and around the blue wool. Their fingers got stiff with cold even though they took turns holding them over the warm register while the other crocheted. They had almost three inches of the scarf done when they heard Ma's voice at the foot of the stairs.

"What are you girls doing up there? It's time to start chores."

Laughing and smiling, Annie and Sally came down. They did not have to answer Ma because it was a Christmas surprise.

During the next week, Annie could spend hardly any time crocheting on the scarf. By the time she got home from school it was getting dark and Ma would not let them work upstairs with a lighted lamp. Sally crocheted a little every afternoon while Ma took a rest, but still the scarf was only about a foot long.

On Saturday, Annie went to help Grandmother, as she had promised. There was a big pile of matted wool in the center of the kitchen table. First, Grandmother took out the carding combs. She poured a little oil over some of the wool, tore off a fistful, and pressed it onto the sharp teeth of the bottom comb. Then she began to pull the top comb over the wool. The metal teeth screeched and scraped against each other.

"This is worse than grinding sickles," said Annie, covering her ears.

"Don't you want to try it?" asked Grandmother.

"I'd rather do the spinning," said Annie. She had tried it once or twice before, last winter. The yarn got full of knobby lumps then, but she was a year older now. She was sure she could do it right.

Grandmother back-combed the wool on the carding comb and it came off in a long piece, shaped almost like a large, limp carrot. Deftly she twisted one end around the spindle and began to press down on the foot pedal that turned the wheel. The spindle whirled, twisting and spinning the wool until it was stretched out and taut, like a long, thick thread. Grandmother kept adding wool until the length of yarn was a few feet out. Then she swung it out and around to the right and wound it on the corncob stuck on the spindle.

"Now it's your turn." Grandmother turned to Annie. "Remember to pedal evenly, and to hold the wool tight, but not too tight. Don't let it go out too fast—that's what makes the lumps."

Annie tried it and right away a thick bump appeared on the yarn; it was twisted and would not pull out. Grandmother guided her hand for a few moments.

"Try to feel it," she said. "Soon you will be able to tell just how it should pull away to give you a nice, even strand."

Annie practiced and practiced, while Grandmother went back to her carding. She was still getting lumpy spots on almost every turn. Just when she felt ready to give up and ask Grandmother if she could do something else, Annie felt a long thread spin smoothly out under her fingers. It twisted and turned in a long even line. There was not a single lump in it.

"I did it!" she cried, but just at that moment, as she fed more wool toward the spindle, a fat knob appeared in the yarn.

"Keep at it," said Grandmother; "I know you will feel it soon."

Sure enough, before long Annie could pedal smoothly and let the wool out evenly, so that very few lumps showed up in the yarn. She filled the cob on the spindle and Grandmother took it off, putting on an empty corncob in its place. Annie felt a stiffness spreading all through her back and shoulders, but she kept up the spinning, while Grandmother continued to card.

At last it was time to stop for dinner. Annie's arms and hands were so tired from holding the wool out taut and straight, they trembled as she set the dinner table. She would never be able to keep spinning all afternoon.

As soon as they had finished dinner, Grandmother smiled at Annie.

"Run along home, now. That's enough for today. Besides, you have to work on the scarf."

Gratefully, Annie skipped off. Now she could crochet most of the afternoon. That was a lot easier than spinning!

Luckily, they had no school from now until after Christmas. Every day she and Sally slipped upstairs to work on the scarf. It was getting longer and longer.

The following Saturday she went to help Grandmother again, but this time they only carded and spun for half of the morning. The rest of the time Annie helped Grandmother with her baking. She was making peppernuts and Annie had to shape and place them on the baking sheets, then take them off again as fast as they came from the oven. After dinner, Grandmother gave her a tin pail full of peppernuts to take home. Ma did not let them eat any. They had to be saved for Christmas, which was only a week away.

Now they rushed to get the house cleaned and cookies baked and their best clothes washed and pressed and ironed. Every moment they could, Sally and Annie crocheted frantically on the blue scarf. They were coming to the last ball of wool.

"Do you think we should use it all?" asked Annie.

"It won't be long enough unless we do," answered Sally.

Not until the day before Christmas Eve did Sally pull the last stitches through, and finish off the end. She wound the scarf around Annie's head and then around her neck. It felt soft and warm.

"Just the right length, I think," said Sally with satisfaction. They could hardly wait to give it to Ma.

On Christmas Eve, Ma scattered straw on the table to remind them that Jesus was born in a stable. Over the straw she spread a white cloth.

"Use the good dishes," she said to Annie, who was about to set the table.

Before they ate their meal, Father brought out the

Christmas wafer they had received in church on the last Sunday of Advent. Solemnly he broke off a piece and passed it to Mother, wishing her a holy and blessed Christmas. Then Ma passed the wafer to each of the children in turn, and they each broke off a tiny piece and ate it.

They could not eat meat that day, but still they feasted, on boiled potatoes with cream gravy, herring with onions, smoked carp, fried mushrooms and pickled red beets. To finish their supper, Ma gave them each a small bowl of peppernuts, over which they poured fresh, cold milk to make them soft.

Hardly had they done drying the dishes when there was a stomping of feet at the door and a jingling of bells.

"The *gvjozdki!*" shrieked Annie. She remembered them from last year. They brought gifts, just like Santa Claus did for other children. But first she would have to prove she had been a good girl.

Pa opened the door and in walked four *gvjozdki*, each one dressed in a different costume. One had a mask with a long, red nose. He wore a long black garment like a priest, and carried a tin can with some coins in it. The second was covered from head to foot in a cape of woven straw. Only his eyes peeped out from between the strands at the top. A third had a suit made of brown fur. On his feet and hands were fur boots and fur mittens with bells at the ankles and wrists, and over his head was a cap and mask also fashioned from some sort of fur. He looked like a big, brown bear walking on its hind legs. On his back he carried a sack.

But it was the fourth *gvjozdka* that made a shiver of suspense pass through Annie and her little brothers. He was not nearly as tall as the others, but he was scarier.

111

His shiny red suit buttoned up like long underwear, but instead of stopping at his neck it went all around his head and over the top part of his face like a tight-fitting stocking cap. Attached to the top were two curved and pointy horns. Hanging from the seat of his pants was a long tail, made from a horse whip, that he twirled in his hands.

"Well, now, who has been bad all year?" asked the red *gvjozdka* in a thin, whispery voice.

Annie and Sally and the boys were silent. They could only stare at the strange costumes.

"What about you, Leo and August? Have you been trying to be naughty, the way you should?"

The two boys shook their heads emphatically.

"You mean to say you always *try* to be *good*?"

The boys nodded, and the red *gvjozdka* twirled his leather tail and gnashed his teeth.

"Grrr," he growled in disgust. "Guess I won't get to use my whip yet." One by one he turned to the other children to ask them the same questions, twirling his tail in anticipation. Each time he got the same answers and would groan and growl in disappointment.

"The children in this family are just too good for me. I have to get out of here," squeaked the red *gvjozdka* in a screechy voice. He did a funny dance all around the room, twirling his tail, and then went out the door.

Then the furry *gvjozdka* took out of his sack an orange, a bag of candy and a wrapped present for each of the children. Annie was about to tear the wrapping off hers when the furry *gvjozdka* turned to Ma and said: "You must have been a good girl, too!"

"What do you mean?" asked Ma with a laugh. Annie could see she was blushing a little.

"One of my helpers told me these good little girls of yours have been making a surprise for you."

Annie almost dropped her presents. How could the *gvjozdka* know that? Could Sally have told him? No, Sally was looking as surprised as she was.

"Yes, yes! They have something for you," said the *gvjozdka*, and he motioned for Sally to go and get it. Sally ran upstairs and came back in a moment with Ma's scarf, wrapped in white paper.

113

"Here it is, Ma. Annie and I made it together."

Ma was speechless. All she could do was stroke the soft wool.

"I think there's even another package here for you," said the *gvjozdka*, pulling out a long, flat box tied with a gold string.

Ma still could not say a word. She opened the box and lifted out a pair of black leather gloves.

"Oh, Ma, they're lined with fur," said Sally.

Ma put them on and they fit exactly.

"Now you shouldn't suffer from the cold," said Pa. Annie saw Ma look at him with a special smile.

At last Ma recovered from her surprise. "I can't be the only one enjoying my presents. Open yours," she directed the children.

Joe had a pocket watch in his box and Sally's contained a book. John's round, fat present turned out to be a baseball and when Annie opened her package she found a red, hard-rubber ball and eight shining metal jacks. They were resting on top of a box of colored pencils. Roman and Leo and August each got a spinning top and a ball.

Later that night, when they came upstairs after returning from Midnight Mass, Annie turned to Sally.

"How do you suppose the *gvjozdka* knew about the scarf?"

"I don't know," said Sally, and suddenly she grinned.

"You *do* know," accused Annie. "Tell me!"

"Really, truly, I don't," insisted Sally.

"But you have an inkling?"

"Maybe," was all Sally would say. Annie had to go to sleep wondering how the *gvjozdka* knew about their secret of the scarf.

Picture Puzzles

On Christmas Day, Grandmother and Grandfather came for dinner. In her arms, Grandmother carried a small bundle of packages. When the children tore them open, out tumbled something red.

"Mittens!" cried Annie. "That's why you needed the red wool."

"Look inside," said Grandmother.

Annie held one of the mitten openings apart.

"It's blue inside. How did you do that, Grandmother?"

"You said the red wool was scratchy, so I double-knit the rest of the lambs' wool inside the red. Now your mittens will be extra warm and they won't feel itchy."

Soon it was time to sit down and eat the roast goose and stuffing, the potato dumplings with gravy, the sweet and sour cabbage, the spiced crabapples, and afterward, poppy seed balls and cake. All afternoon, and the next day as well, Ma left the cookies and cakes on the table and they could eat as many as they wanted. After the long days of Advent when they were not allowed to eat any sweets, the days of Christmas seemed like one endless, sugary dream to Annie.

Two days after Christmas, they got their first heavy snowstorm. It snowed for a day and a night.

"If this keeps up, you will have to go to Latsch Valley school for a while," said Ma. "You could never walk to Pine Creek in all this snow."

Annie knew that was the school on Tushner's corner. A few of the families sent their children there, because they thought Pine Creek was too far away.

"I suppose I won't get to Winona after all," Sally sighed. She had intended to take the train on Wednesday.

"I think the track should be clear by then and I have to take the cream in to Dodge anyway, so you should get off on time," said Pa. He was right, because by Wednesday the roads were pretty clear.

"Goodbye!" called Sally as she went out the door. "I'll be back in two weeks."

On the weekend it snowed again. They could not get to church; the wind was blowing the snow in drifts so high that the horses could not get through. Finally, on Tuesday, the weather was cold but clear.

John and Annie struggled through the deep drifts of the valley road. In many places, the snow came to their waists. The small schoolhouse was only a mile away but it took almost as long to get there as it took to walk to Pine Creek on a pleasant day.

Annie hesitated outside the door.

"Don't be scared," said John. "We're all in the same room here." He opened the door and they walked into a room filled with desks. Most of them were already occupied by children of all sizes. At the teacher's desk in front stood a short, pretty lady with light brown hair.

"That's Miss McCabe," whispered John. "I had her two years ago."

"Don't we have a Sister for a teacher?" asked Annie softly, so no one around her could hear.

"No, you silly goose. This is a public school." John laughed at her as though she should have known that.

At nine o'clock the teacher rang a small bell and called the children to order.

"I see many new faces today," she said. "My name is Miss Molly McCabe and when I finish calling the roll, I want those whose names I did not call to raise their hands."

There were only fourteen names on the regular roll call, so more than a dozen children raised their hands at the end. One by one, Miss McCabe asked them to stand and say their names. Then she asked them what reader they were in.

She made some of the children move to other desks, so they would be near those who were on the same level. It did not look at all like the classroom in Pine Creek school. Here there were some big boys and girls sitting toward the front with the smaller children, and a few smaller children sitting way at the back.

Miss McCabe was kept busy moving back and forth among the desks, listening to the different reading groups, watching the advanced pupils do long division at the blackboard, and generally keeping an eye on the whole room so that none of the children could start acting up. She didn't do things the way Sister Pelagia did.

"I was just getting used to first grade in Pine Creek school," thought Annie, "and now I have to learn how to be a first-grader all over again."

At recess and dinnertime, it was so cold the children went out for only a few minutes and came back in again. The younger ones sat at their desks, eating from their dinner pails. The older ones clustered around the stove at the back of the room. Annie could see John standing at the edge of the group. They began to talk in Polish, laughing and giggling at what they said.

Annie gasped. They were saying bad things about Miss McCabe!

Miss McCabe looked up from her desk. She got up and slowly walked toward Annie. In the back of the room one of the boys was whispering in Polish. Annie did not hear exactly what he said but she did hear the shocked gasps and guffaws of the others standing around him.

"Annie, what did he say?" asked Miss McCabe.

Without realizing what she was doing, Annie answered in Polish, saying: "I didn't hear him."

"I asked you a question in English, Annie. Please answer me in English. I don't understand Polish." Miss McCabe's voice was trembly and choked, as though she might break into tears any moment.

Annie simply gaped at her. Not understand Polish! She had never heard of such a person. Why, everyone in their valley and around Pine Creek could talk in Polish.

"Annie, I asked you a question," repeated Miss Mc-Cabe. *"What did he say?"* She spoke each word loudly and slowly and clearly. The back of the room was now silent.

Annie came out of her daze.

"I didn't hear, Miss McCabe, honest, I didn't."

"Very well," said Miss McCabe. "I have only one recourse. In this school we speak English. If you wish to speak Polish then you must go to Pine Creek school or stay home. The next one to say a word in Polish will be sent home immediately."

"That isn't fair," thought Annie. Sometimes she could only think of the Polish way to say things. It was hard to remember certain words in English. Everyone else in the classroom could understand. Why couldn't Miss McCabe learn Polish?

For the rest of that day, the children were quiet. They were all afraid of saying a word in Polish, by accident. No one wanted to get sent home because they knew their parents would take the side of the teacher, who must always be obeyed. They would get a punishment, probably a spanking or a strapping.

In mid-January, Sally returned from Winona. She had had to stay an extra week because of a bad storm. Sally did not go to Latsch Valley school. "It would not help me to keep up with the lessons for seventh grade in Pine Creek," she said, "so I might as well stay here and help Ma."

Through all the long, snowy January days there was order in the valley school. Everyone was quiet. Some of the older children were no longer coming to school.

"I wonder if they walk every day to Pine Creek," thought Annie. She wished she could go back there, too. Sister Pelagia was strict, but not as strict as Miss McCabe.

Instead of going away, the snow got deeper and deeper from more storms. One day in early February, the children were sitting at their desks at noontime, eating from their dinner pails. Miss McCabe sat at her desk reading a newspaper. The older children finished as quickly as they could and went outside. They did not like to stay inside unless they were forced to. Suddenly, Miss McCabe spoke loudly.

"Who would like to come up and work a puzzle?" she asked. "There is a prize for the one who can solve it first."

The children sat up and looked at Miss McCabe when she said the word "prize."

"I would like to get a prize," thought Annie to herself.

"What kind of puzzle is it?" asked Florence.

"A picture puzzle," replied Miss McCabe with a smile.

Slowly, some of the children left their seats and edged towards the front. Annie joined them. Before long, they surrounded Miss McCabe's desk, peering at the newspaper page.

"See this picture? You must find a rabbit hidden somewhere in it," said Miss McCabe.

Annie stared and stared at the picture. It showed a wintry scene of a house and tree and garden, with a man standing in front. Nowhere could she see a rabbit in the picture. In fact, she could see no animal at all.

"You must look very closely, and from all directions," instructed Miss McCabe. "If you do find it, don't point or say it out loud. Whisper it in my ear, so the others can have a chance to guess."

The children looked and looked, taking turns at different sides of the desk to see the picture from every angle.

"I see it," cried Florence. "It's in the—"

"Sssh!" interrupted Miss McCabe. "Whisper it to me."

Florence whispered something to Miss McCabe, who nodded her had. "That's correct. That's where it is."

Now Annie looked harder. Where could Florence see a rabbit? There was just a lot of snow, a house, a bare tree with lots of branches and no leaves—suddenly, Annie stopped her glance. The twigs and branches of the tree seemed to make an eye and a pair of ears in one spot. Could that be where the rabbit was? She moved to a position facing that side of the picture. Yes, there it was, as clear as anything. A rabbit was hiding in the tree branches.

"I see it," she said, just as two others shouted at the same time. Finally, when noon recess was about to end, Miss McCabe asked Florence to point to where the rabbit was, to show the children who still had not seen it.

"Now we will fill in the contest form with your name and address, Florence, and send it in to the Winona *Independent*. They are offering a free subscription for one month to the first ten persons who send in the answer to the puzzle. If we get it in quickly, you might be one of those to get a prize. Every week there will be a different puzzle. See, it's here in their new feature, 'The Children's Page.'"

They looked more closely and saw that the page included a story, a rebus, two poems and the puzzle.

"Oh, why didn't I see that rabbit first," thought Annie. "It would be so much fun to get the newspaper every week." She was jealous of Florence because she had a chance to win it.

Annie had heard Pa and Ma talk about getting a newspaper, now that the mailman came right to their valley. She had heard them call it Rural Free Delivery. That evening, when she came home from school, before she even took her coat off she asked Ma a question.

"Are we going to get the newspaper like you and Pa talked about?"

"One of these days we'll sign up," said Ma.

"Oh, please sign up soon, Ma," begged Annie. "Miss McCabe showed us the newspaper today and it has such a lot of nice things in it."

"I'll ask Pa tonight," promised Ma.

When Pa heard the question he hesitated only for a moment. "I guess we should keep up with the news regular-like. I'll order it the next time I go to Dodge. Mrs. Jereczek should have all the information."

The next time he went to Dodge, Pa announced on his return that he had ordered a newspaper subscription. "It should start coming in about a week," he said.

Impatiently Annie waited, hoping that the first day it came would be the day with the Children's Page. Every evening she hurried home from school to see if it had arrived in the new mailbox Pa had fixed up at the corner where their road joined the valley road. One day when she entered the house, Ma pointed to the kitchen table.

"The first newspaper came today, Annie. But I don't see a Children's Page."

Annie rushed to the table where Ma had spread it out. Carefully, she paged through it, looking at each big sheet. Something did not seem right. She turned to the front page.

"Is this the Winona *Independent*?" she asked.

"Why no," answered Ma. "This is the Winona *Republican Herald*. You never said a thing about which paper it was and Pa ordered this one."

Annie looked at the newspaper in disappointment.

"Maybe this newspaper has a Children's Page, too," said Ma brightly. "We'll watch for it every day."

For a week they scanned the newspaper, looking for puzzles and pictures. But there didn't seem to be a special Children's Page.

"Here's a continued story, called 'Polly of the Circus,'" said Sally. "I'll read that to you every evening."

"I want a puzzle page," said Annie with a pout.

"Well, I'm sorry but there isn't one," said Ma sadly. "Pa signed up for a year and it costs a lot of money to have it sent, so I'm sure he'll say we have to stick with this one."

That week Miss McCabe brought another of her newspapers to school.

"Would anyone like to work on the puzzle again?" she asked, when they had finished eating.

"I would!" Annie jumped up from her seat and hurried to the desk. Perhaps if she got to see the picture first, she would figure it out ahead of everyone else.

"This week it is a hard puzzle," announced Miss McCabe to the children assembled around her desk. "I must confess I haven't found the answer myself. Here, let me read you the instructions: 'Billy Bodkins is going to take Susie Smiles for a ride on his sled. Can you find Susie?'"

Annie gazed intently at the picture of a smiling boy pulling his sled. Behind him was a tree, to the right were a lot of bushes, and all around him were heaps of snow.

"I've looked and looked and for the life of me I can't see any girl," said Miss McCabe.

There was absolute silence in the room as they all stared hard at the picture. Annie felt her eyes start to water. She closed them for a moment and then half opened them, blinking a little. Then she opened them wide. Was that a girl's head in Billy's sweater? She blinked again. Yes, it was.

"I see her!" Annie shrieked, jumping up and down. "I see her!" She whispered the answer in Miss McCabe's ear.

"Yes, yes. Now I see her, too," replied Miss McCabe.

None of the other pupils could find Susie Smiles. They looked and looked but the more they searched, the less they were able to see anything like a girl's shape in the puzzle picture. At last, Annie showed them.

"Would you like me to fill out the contest form?" asked Miss McCabe. "Florence did not win because we were too late in sending the answer, but this paper arrived today and the puzzle is so difficult, I think you might have a chance."

Annie wanted to send in the contest form, but she wanted to fill it out herself. She knew how to write her name quite clearly.

"*Proszę*," she said, which means "Please" in Polish. "I want to do it myself."

The moment she said it, Annie realized what she had done. She had spoken a word in Polish, and now Miss McCabe would send her home, without giving her a chance to fill in the contest form.

"I didn't mean to, Miss McCabe," apologized Annie.

"Didn't mean to what?" inquired the teacher.

"To say a word in Polish."

"Oh, that!" laughed Miss McCabe. "Even *I* know that means 'Please.' That isn't what I meant about talking Polish."

"But you said the next one to say a word in Polish would get sent home."

Miss McCabe looked astonished.

"I see there has been a misunderstanding," she said at last. "I didn't mean words like 'Please' or 'Thank you' or things like that. I *like* to learn such words in Polish. I meant that you should not say things I cannot under-stand—whole phrases or sentences—and then laugh about it. That's not polite. You wouldn't like it if I spoke

125

about you in another language and you could not understand, would you?"

Annie shook her head.

"We'll discuss this further when the other pupils come back. Now, let's fill out the contest form."

Neatly, Annie wrote her name on the top line. Then she hesitated. What was she supposed to write in the second line? She had never written out her address before, so she didn't know what it was.

"Print 'R' period, 'F' period, 'D' period," prompted Miss McCabe. "That stands for Rural Free Delivery. And this valley is on Route Number One, so put a comma and the number one after R.F.D. Do you know your box number?"

Again Annie shook her head. Then she had an idea.

"I think maybe John knows. When he comes in I can ask him."

"Very well. Write 'B-o-x' and leave a space for the number after it. On the last line you must write 'Dodge, Wisconsin.'" Miss McCabe spelled it all out for her. Annie completed the form and then Miss McCabe gave her an envelope. She had to copy from the newspaper the long address of the Winona *Independent*.

"Do you have two pennies?" asked Miss McCabe.

"I have five pennies at home," replied Annie.

"I'll put a stamp on, then, and you must bring me two pennies tomorrow to pay for it."

When John came in, he told them their box number was 62, so Annie filled in the space. Then Miss McCabe called the class to order and explained about the Polish misunderstanding. Everyone felt relieved now that they didn't have to worry about saying a Polish word accidentally.

"I'm going to like Latsch Valley school after all,"

thought Annie.

But that weekend Pa said the roads were clearing up nicely and they could go back to Pine Creek school on Monday. Annie was disappointed because now she would not see Miss McCabe again, but Ma reassured her.

"You will probably get to the valley school for a month or two again next winter. I am sure Miss McCabe will still be there."

One day, soon after that, Annie came home from school and found Ma smiling at her.

"A card came for you today, Annie."

"The contest!" Annie knew it had to be that. Ma handed her a postcard with an announcement on the back:

> We are pleased to inform you that your solution to the Children's Page Picture Puzzle was one of the first ten to reach our offices during the week of *February* 8-12, 1909 . You will be receiving a free month's subscription to the Winona *Independent* commencing next week. We hope you and your family will enjoy the many features of our fine newspaper and that you will continue to be a subscriber in the months and years to come.

After Ma read it aloud and explained what it meant, she gave it to Annie to keep.

"You must save it carefully, in your bureau drawer. We'll show it to both grandmothers and grandfathers, the near ones and the far ones. They will be pleased to see what a clever girl you are."

That made Annie happy, but she was looking forward to something even nicer.

"I'll get to do all the puzzles first because it will be my very own newspaper. At least for a month."

Lent

Late in February the whole family went to church on Ash Wednesday. All of them, even Roman and Leo and August, marched up to the Communion rail and knelt down. There they waited while the priest dipped his thumb in a bowl of ashes and then pressed it against each of their foreheads in turn, making a sign in the shape of a cross.

Leo didn't like it and tried to brush the ashes away, but Ma held on to his hands. Soon he forgot all about them.

That was the start of Lent, so now they had to think about special sacrifices they could make. There would be no more cakes or cookies or sweets to eat until Easter.

"And try not to eat so much between meals, Anienka," chided Ma. "It won't be too many years before you make your First Holy Communion, so you must learn to fast little by little."

"I get so hungry," sighed Annie. She knew that grown-ups were not supposed to eat between meals during Lent, and whenever they wanted to go to Communion, they didn't eat breakfast that morning. But every time she tried to stay away from food between meals, she got hungrier and hungrier, just thinking about it. John was preparing for his First Communion later that year, and he also had a hard time fasting.

"I know it is hard," answered Ma. "But we all have to learn."

In the evenings during Lent, Ma always brought out feathers to strip, and while they all sat around the table tearing the quills off, Pa read from the Polish *Book of the Saints.* Annie liked hearing some of the stories, especially the ones about the saints who were kings and queens, like King Kazimir and Queen Kunigunda and Queen Matilda. Sometimes what Pa read was so unusual, Annie forgot to strip feathers and began to daydream instead.

On March 7, he read about St. Thomas Aquinas.

"You dumb ox," St. Thomas's classmates had called him, because he seemed so stupid. And yet he had turned out to be smart after all.

"Some of the boys in my class are dumb," thought Annie. "I wonder if any are really smart, only we don't know it yet?"

On March 9, it was the feast of St. Frances of Rome.

"'At the age of eleven years,'" read Pa, "'sweet, virtuous Frances was married to a nobleman.'"

"Eleven years!" exclaimed Annie.

"That's what it says, eleven years," repeated Pa.

"Goodness," thought Annie, "that is two years younger than Sally is now." She wanted to ask Sally if it would feel strange to be married, but she dared not interrupt Pa's reading again.

They always ended the evening with hymns, led by Pa in his deep, bass voice. Ma sang the higher part, with Annie and the boys joining her, while Sally and Joe sang the lower harmony.

Every night, after the stories and singing, Annie felt so inspired she would always go to bed thinking: "Tomorrow I am going to be really, truly good. I won't eat between meals and I won't quarrel with the boys." But almost always she broke her resolve, and found herself arguing with John or Roman, or eating a piece of bread and butter after school, because she was just too hungry to wait for supper.

"It's so easy to *want* to do the right thing," thought Annie, "but so hard to do it."

In the last week in March, two weeks before Easter, Ma and Pa announced they were going to Winona again.

"This time we'll take all the boys. I don't like you missing a day of school, John, but this is our only chance to buy your First Communion suit," said Ma.

"Who will stay home and mind the farm?" asked Annie.

"It can mind itself for one day," laughed Pa. "We'll be sure to be back by three or four. The chores can wait until then."

The next morning a light drizzle was coming down.

"You might as well ride with us as far as the Pine Creek turnoff," said Ma to Sally and Annie. "We'll be leaving about the same time as you."

Annie was glad they could get a ride. It was no fun walking to school in the rain. Sometimes their coats and shawls got so wet they did not dry out completely during the long school day. Then they had to put them back on even though they still felt damp and cold. Riding in the buggy, they could cover up with an old blanket, so they hardly got wet at all.

At the turnoff, Annie and Sally jumped down and continued on foot while the buggy headed for Winona. All through the school day, Annie imagined them driving up and across the bridge, and through the streets of Winona. In the afternoon, the weather cleared and it became a lovely spring day.

On the way home, Annie did not feel like walking fast to keep up with Sally and her friends. She dawdled along with Vic and Damazy and Alex and Martin. They stopped every now and then to look at things in the marshes and pools next to the roadside, things like grass snakes and frogs and salamanders and turtles. The melting snow and rain had made the fields too wet to walk across, so they had to take the longer road home, instead of the short-cuts.

At the valley road turnoff, Alex and Martin kept going on the main road, but Annie and Vic and Damazy turned to the right. Far ahead, they could see Sally and the girls rounding a curve in the road. Sometimes they were lucky and could catch a ride on the wagon of one of the valley farmers returning home from Dodge, but today there was no vehicle in sight.

"I wish we could get a ride," sighed Annie. She was tired from the long walk, especially since she had not eaten anything since dinnertime.

"We just missed somebody," said Vic. "See the fresh

horse and buggy tracks?"

Annie looked down at the muddy road. Yes, there were the hoof marks and the wheel lines, so sharp and clear they could only have been made less than an hour earlier.

"It must have been Pa and Ma," she cried, starting to run. "If only I had walked faster," she thought, "I would have gotten a ride with them." She hurried so much, she felt a stitch of pain in her side and had to slow down. At last she came to the place where their road branched off and curved up and around to the house and farmyard.

"They probably picked up the mail," said Annie to herself, but she decided to check the mailbox anyway. Her newspaper had stopped coming a few days ago, but she kept hoping that somehow they would forget about the month being up, and continue sending it to her.

She unhooked the door of the mailbox and pulled it down. No, nothing there. But just as she closed the door and dropped the hook into the eyehole screw, she spied a brown paper bag at the bottom of the ditch below the mailbox.

"That bag looks new," thought Annie. Carefully, she climbed down through the rocks and mud until she could reach out and grab it. It was covered with splatters of mud, but the paper was so strong the contents had not broken through. The top was twisted tightly shut. Cautiously Annie opened it.

"Oh!" she gasped the moment she looked inside. "Easter candy!" The bag was full of colored jelly beans, gumdrops and tiny pastel hearts with writing on them.

"I wonder who dropped the bag here?" Annie asked herself. A Voice deep inside her tried to answer, "Ma must have dropped it," but Annie pretended not to hear. She opened her empty dinner pail and stuffed the brown bag inside.

"If I sneak it upstairs and hide it under the bed," thought Annie, "I can have all the candy I want, whenever I want it."

"You can't do that—that would be stealing," said the Voice, but Annie still ignored it.

"Finders keepers, losers weepers," she chanted aloud, and started walking up the road to the house.

"If you keep the candy, Sally and the boys will get none," said the Voice, and this time Annie paid attention to it. Sally was always so good to her—it wouldn't be fair not to give her some.

"I'll give some to Sally," Annie answered the Voice. "I'll tell her I found it." But then she could picture the disappointment in the boys' eyes on Easter Sunday morning, when they found no candy by their plates.

"I'll give some to the boys, too," thought Annie.

"You must give it all to Ma," said the Voice.

"I could empty some of the candy out in my pail and give the paper bag to Ma. She would never know I took some out. She would just think it got lost in the ditch."

During the entire walk up to the house, Annie argued with the Voice inside her, over whether she should give all the candy to Ma, to share with everyone, or whether she should keep some in secret, just for herself. She arrived at the door and reluctantly opened it.

"I can't imagine how I could have left it behind," Ma was saying to Sally. "I'm sure Mr. Libera put it in my basket, right on top."

"Maybe it fell out somewhere along the way," suggested Sally.

Instantly, Annie knew they were talking about the bag of candy. Now was the moment she had to decide. Should she take it up and hide it until she could safely remove some, or should she give it to Ma right away?

"You didn't happen to see a brown bag along the road, did you?" asked Ma.

Now Annie felt she had no choice. She had to tell the truth.

"Yes, Ma. I found it in the ditch by the mailbox. It's here in my dinner pail."

Ma looked at her in disbelief and then lifted the cover off the pail.

"You really did find it," she said. "It must have slipped out of my basket as I reached to get the mail. Funny, I didn't hear it fall." Ma was still looking at the candy in amazement. Then she leaned over and gave Annie a big hug.

"My clever little girl with the sharp eyes! Now I'll be able to give you an Easter surprise after all, except it won't be much of a surprise for you, will it?"

Annie squirmed. Usually she liked it when Ma hugged her, but this time the Voice inside her was saying accusingly: "You don't deserve a hug. If Ma had not asked you about the bag, would you have told her about it right away?" And Annie could not answer the Voice, because the truth was she did not *know* whether she would have tried to sneak the bag upstairs if Ma had not asked that question just as she came in the door.

"But I *am* glad she asked it," Annie answered the Voice, and she gave Ma a big hug in return.

Fancy Feather

"Will it come soon, Pa?" asked Annie, for at least the fifth time.

"Pretty soon," answered Pa.

It was Easter Monday and they were waiting at the train depot in Dodge. Aunt Pauline, Ma's sister, was coming to visit for a week. Annie had been allowed to go along in the wagon to meet her. First Pa had taken the cream to the creamery. Then he had bought a few groceries for Ma. And then they had been waiting all morning.

Just as she was about to ask once more if the train would come soon, she heard the long, hooting whistle of the engine in the distance.

"It's coming, at last!"

"Should be here in about five minutes." Pa looked at his watch.

The whistle sounded again. Then the engine could be heard, chuffing softly at the far end of Dodge. At last it pulled into the depot, making a lot of noise as it screeched to a halt.

Not many people got off. Aunt Pauline appeared at the top of the steps and the trainman helped her down.

"Don't you look all spiffed up!" exclaimed Pa. Annie was so dazzled she could not say a word. Never had she seen Aunt Pauline dressed so beautifully. Her deep blue dress was made of silk, puffed at the tops of the sleeves and narrow at the waist. At her neck was an insert of creamy lace. But most unusual of all was the feather on her hat. It was the longest feather Annie had ever seen, and it curved around and swooped to the back; the gentle breeze made it move like a bird, dipping and swaying in a circle.

"Oh, Aunt Pauline, you look as pretty as some of the pictures in my newspaper," breathed Annie.

"Well, now," said Pa very seriously to Annie. "Do you think she will be ashamed to ride with us on the wagon seat? Maybe we should hire a livery here in Dodge? And that feather looks mighty dangerous. Why, it might hook itself right around a fellow's neck if he got too close."

"Stop your teasing, John," said Aunt Pauline. She was blushing pinkly. "It's the latest fashion, and I have to be fashionable if I want to get sewing orders from the ladies of society. You know as well as anyone that I'm not ashamed to ride on any wagon, so long as it's clean. Why, I rode with you many a time when Annie was a baby. You certainly remember the time we took her to be baptized, don't you?"

"Tell me about it," pleaded Annie. She knew the story but she liked to hear it again and again.

"I was living at your house then, helping your mother," said Aunt Pauline. "That was before I learned dressmaking. Why, I was only fourteen!" she paused to think for a while.

"Go on," prodded Annie.

"Your mother was so frightened she was going to lose you. Then when you came, you were such a nice, big, healthy baby. But you just would not cry. Right after you were born, you gave a funny cough, but you did not cry out the way most babies do. Your mother was positive you would not live long. So she insisted you had to be baptized right away, the day after you were born. Your Pa and I didn't want to take you out so soon, but I do believe your Ma would have got up on the wagon herself and taken you, if we hadn't; she was so insistent. So I held on to you while your Pa took care of the cream cans, and off we went. You were as quiet as a rabbit—you still had not cried one little bit." Aunt Pauline paused for a moment.

"Then what happened, Pa?" asked Annie.

"First, we dropped off the cream in Dodge, and then we went to Pine Creek. I was sure you would start crying soon, because your Ma wasn't there to feed you."

"And then?"

"Then we had to wait for the priest to get finished with his breakfast," continued Aunt Pauline. "By that time, I was getting frightened, too. You were so still and quiet. At last the priest came out and we went into the church. It was cool inside. He started the prayers and there still wasn't a peep out of you."

"Then the priest brought out the pitcher of water,

didn't he?" asked Annie. She liked this part of the story best.

"That he did," answered Aunt Pauline. "He poured that cool water over your head and started to say 'I baptize you . . . ' but you let out such a piercing shriek that he almost dropped the pitcher—and I almost dropped you," laughed Aunt Pauline.

"And what did you say, Pa?"

"That you were sure to scare the devil away with that shrieking and screaming—that's what I said. And didn't Father Gara agree with me? You bet he did. He said he hadn't heard such a noise in ten years of baptizing. Yes, sir! That devil would never dare to show himself near there again."

"Oh, Pa, there's no devil in church," laughed Annie.

"That's because you scared him off," said Pa solemnly, but Annie saw him wink at Aunt Pauline.

All the rest of the way home they talked and laughed about the time when Annie was a little girl and the things she did. Soon they were pulling up in front of the house. Ma stepped outside to welcome her sister.

"Pauline, you surely do sew a fine seam. I have never seen such an elegant dress! And where did you get that feather?" Ma looked Pauline up and down, and then walked around her, admiring the dress from the back as well as the front. Sally looked closely at the dress, too, and stroked the smooth fabric.

"How lovely it is. Do you have any other dresses like it?" she asked.

"I have one or two more I made last fall," answered Aunt Pauline. "I've been much too busy sewing for others in the weeks before Easter to get any more done up for myself."

Later that day, Aunt Pauline showed them the other two fine dresses she had brought with her. Last of all, she took from her bag a soft pile of deep blue cloth.

"This is for you, Sis. I'm going to make a dress out of it, just for you."

Ma gasped with delight.

"Pauline, this will be much too fancy for me," she protested. Annie could see that her cheeks were glowing and her eyes sparkling.

"Nonsense," said Aunt Pauline. "I insist you take it and I don't want to hear another word against it. I'll start cutting it out tomorrow."

During the week, Aunt Pauline sewed a little on the dress every day. Most of the time she spent quietly chatting with Ma. By Saturday morning, though, the dress was finished except for the hem. Ma tried it on and Aunt Pauline measured the hemline so it was a few inches off the floor all around, except in the back, where it was supposed to touch the floor in a short train.

"There! Another hour and it will be finished. Tomorrow you can wear it to church."

"Oh, I couldn't do that," said Ma. "I think I should wait for a wedding or something special."

"I don't see why you can't wear it to church on Sunday. You didn't have a new dress for Easter, did you? So this can be your Easter dress, a week late." Aunt Pauline's voice was firm and insistent.

"Oh, please, Ma, wear it," begged Annie. "You look so pretty in it."

"I think you should wear it," said Sally quietly.

Ma looked all around at her admirers.

"All right, I'll wear it! But won't people think it funny that I saved my new dress for a week *after* Easter!" Ma laughed merrily.

The next morning Ma put on the new dress. Then she brought out her old black hat with the black silk ribbon. She looked at it with a sigh, and started to put it on.

"You can't wear *that* hat!" cried Aunt Pauline. "Here, I'll let you have mine, with the feather. It picks up the blue so well. I'll wear my other hat with the green ribbon." Before Ma could protest at all, Aunt Pauline had placed the hat on Ma's head and pinned it in place. The feather bobbed and swayed saucily.

Pa came out of the bedroom where he had been getting dressed up for church.

"Well, well! So you don't want to catch a fellow with that feather after all," he teased Aunt Pauline.

"Hush, John! Stop your teasing. How does it look?" asked Ma.

"Mighty fancy! Mighty fancy! I think I'll have to go and change my tie for the silk one I use at weddings." Pa chuckled and went back to the bedroom.

"Oh, Pauline, it feels so strange on my head. Are you sure it looks all right?" Ma had a doubtful frown on her face.

"It looks lovely. Just hold your head up high and keep your chin tucked in. That way it will stay beautifully balanced."

All the way to church, Annie could not take her eyes away from the feather. It bounced and waved in the spring breezes. The boys kept eyeing it as well. When they arrived at church, Ma turned to the girls.

"Sally, you and Annie sit in the pew behind us. With the boys and Pauline, we'll fill up our pew."

During Mass, Annie could hardly concentrate. She kept watching the feather. Sometimes, if Ma moved her head quickly to the side, the feather would almost poke Pa in the eye.

"Oh," gasped Annie, barely managing to cover the sound with her hand. The feather had touched Pa on the cheek! Annie looked around carefully. A lot of people seemed to have their eyes on the feather, instead of on Father Gara and the altar.

At last it was Communion time. Pa, Ma, Aunt Pauline

and Joe got up from their pew to go to the altar rail. Sally stood up and followed them.

"I hope Ma holds her head up straight," thought Annie. All during Communion she worried whether the feather would poke someone.

Around to the side and back into the pews they walked, with their eyes cast down and hands folded. Sally knelt down, closed her eyes and said her after-Communion prayers. In the pew ahead, Ma and Pa and the others were doing the same.

Father Gara finished passing out the Communion wafers and then began to cleanse and wipe out the chalice. It was quiet and still in the church. Suddenly, Ma leaned back in the pew. Sometimes she got tired of kneeling too long, and sat back while the others knelt.

Annie watched the feather as it swayed softly. It was only a short distance away from Sally's nose, because she was kneeling directly behind Ma. Sally continued to pray, eyes tightly closed and hands folded in front.

"Oh, please, Ma, don't move," prayed Annie silently. But Ma did not hear that silent prayer. Quickly but gently she slid back on to the seat. The tip of the feather curled around the lower part of Sally's nose.

"Eeek!" she squealed, so loudly that everyone around jumped. Ma turned completely around and so did Pa. This time Pa's chin moved directly in the path of the feather. Without realizing what he was doing, he brushed it away with his hand, as though brushing away an insect. The hat tipped crazily over Ma's forehead.

Joe and John started snickering and so did most of the other people seated around them. Ma flushed red in embarrassment as she tried to straighten the hat. From the altar, Father Gara peered down to see what the commotion was all about.

Finally, amid the sound of snuffles and titters, he said the final blessing and marched out with the altar servers. At last they could leave the church.

"Hoo, hoo!" hooted Pa with laughter as they came outside. "I thought that feather would get me after all."

"Oh, Ma, I'm sorry," apologized Sally. "I didn't hear you slide back. I didn't mean to scream like that. It just came out."

"Never mind," said Ma, starting to take off the hat. "It wasn't your fault. Pauline, you are going to have to take this hat back with you. I would never get used to it. It's a hat for a city lady, not for me."

"Keep the hat, Sis," pleaded Aunt Pauline. "I'll take off the feather so it won't bother you."

"No," laughed Ma, shaking her head. "I'd be too ashamed to wear it around here again. Everyone would take one look at it and wonder what I did with that fancy feather. Why, they'd probably have to laugh just thinking about it. I do." And Ma broke into peals of laughter.

"I Want to Be a Married Man"

Aunt Pauline left on Monday, taking the feather hat with her. The next Sunday Ma wore her new dress again because Rogation Day fell on Sunday that year and they always wore their best clothes for the procession. The new seeds got blessed and this time Pa and Ma made no mention of leaving the farm.

Then the cows started to come in fresh. Every few days in May there was a newborn calf in the barn. By the end of the month they had twelve new calves.

"With all this fresh milk and cream, I think it's time I made some *sara*," said Ma one day at breakfast. Everyone's mouth started to water. Ma made cottage cheese all through the year, but *sara* was their favorite kind of cheese, and Ma made it only when the cows had just given birth to their calves.

That morning Ma put some fresh milk and cream into two large bowls. After Sally had churned the butter, she added buttermilk to the bowls and set them off to the side, on the part of the stove over the warm water tank.

"Don't move them or bump them," Ma warned Annie and the boys.

After two days the milk and cream looked thick and curdled. Ma lined a colander with a piece of white cloth and set it in a pan. Then she poured the creamy curds into the colander. Slowly, the whey began to drip through the cloth into the pan.

"Take it down to the cellar for me, Sally, will you? And cover it over with that oilcloth, nice and tight."

"I'll help you," offered Annie. She cleared a space on the old table in the cellar and Sally put the pan down carefully. Then they draped the oilcloth over the colander and the pan, and put stones all around the edge to hold it in place.

The next morning Ma asked Sally to bring it up again.

"Annie, you can get the baskets ready." Ma brought out cheesecloth and two low baskets that were no bigger around than their dinner plates. Annie spread the cheesecloth in the baskets and smoothed it out so there were no wrinkles on the bottom.

Then Ma salted and peppered the drained curds and spooned them into the baskets, spreading them evenly and pressing them down lightly. She folded the cheesecloth over the tops and set a plate over each basket.

"Now take them down again."

Once more Sally carried the cheese down to the cellar,

only this time she did not set the baskets in a pan. Instead, she placed them side by side on a wire rack on the table. Then she and Annie covered them as before with the oilcloth, leaving a space for the whey to drip through.

The next day the cheese was ready, so for dinner Ma fried potatoes and pulled up the first radishes. She cut the creamy, smooth cheese into thick wedges and put them on slices of bread. Pa sliced his radishes and put them over the cheese, but Annie liked to bite off a big chunk of bread and cheese, then dunk a radish in the mound of salt on her plate and pop it into her mouth. The mellow taste of the cheese and the tangy sharpness of the radish tasted so good she could hardly bring herself to eat any potatoes.

A few weeks later the first lettuce grew tall enough to be cut and they ate the crispy leaves in a cream dressing over boiled potatoes. Later came the new peas, which Ma boiled in their pods. They popped the whole pods into their mouths and then slid them out again, leaving behind the delicately sweet, round peas, to be chewed and swallowed.

Every week it seemed there were new and delicious foods to eat. They came around each year in their season and each year they seemed to be more delectable.

"I always forget how good they all taste," said Annie.

The Sundays of the growing season were also visiting time. Some Sundays Far Grandmother and Grandfather would drive out if the weather was fine and spend the day. Near Grandmother and Grandfather came often, especially on those Sundays when Old Frank and Barney and Mary said they would walk over for the afternoon. Annie could see Pa liked that, because they played cards

147

for a few hours. Pa served the men tall, foaming glasses of beer and Ma brought out her elderberry wine for the ladies.

Aunt Augusta and Uncle Isidore came once with their three children, and twice Uncle Leo and Aunt Anna showed up with their two babies. These were the only first cousins Annie had, and they were all younger than she was. Roman and Leo and August enjoyed playing with them, but Annie preferred it when Pa and Ma and the family were invited to Barney's house, because then she could have fun with Vic and his cousins, who were more her age.

"I can't decide if I like summer or winter better," thought Annie. But as the days grew warmer and longer, Sundays began to have that nice, stretched-out feeling and then Annie would always say: "I like summer best of all."

One Sunday, on the way home from church, Pa stopped at the tavern in Dodge.

"I'll be out in two shakes of a lamb's tail," he said. He was going to pick up another pony of beer to take to Barney's house in the afternoon.

Annie looked around at the other buggies waiting in front of the tavern. Next to theirs was the Wicka family's buggy. The older girls in it sat straight and tall, talking softly to each other. Annie could not hear what they said.

Suddenly, a group of young men came out of the tavern, laughing and singing. Their eyes swept the line-up of buggies. One of the young men put his hands in his pockets, lifted his head, and broke into song:

Chce rozpocząć spokojny żywot małżenski!

I want to be a married man!

As he sang he sauntered up to the Wicka buggy and slowly walked around it. The Wicka girls giggled and blushed.

"Why is he doing that?" Annie whispered to Sally.

"Because he wants to get married and he's hoping one of the girls is sweet on him," answered Sally.

Round and round the buggy went the young man, singing his song over several times. When he got no reply from the girls, he went farther down the line, to another buggy. There was only one girl in it, sitting next to her mother.

"I want to be a married man," crooned the man.

"I want to cuddle up to a man," sang the girl in

answer, harmonizing with the man's voice. They completed the song, alternating lines, and then everyone in all the buggies laughed and clapped.

"What does that mean?" whispered Annie.

"It probably means she would like to get married, too, and that she wouldn't mind if he came calling on her," said Sally in a low voice.

Just at that moment, another young man from the group stepped out and began the same song:

Chce rozpocząć spokojny żywot małżenski!

I want to be a married man!

He strolled in their direction.

"My goodness, he's coming toward us," thought Annie. The young man came up to their buggy; he stopped and began to dance a little jig to his tune, all the while looking up at them.

"Why, he's looking at Sally!" thought Annie. She discovered to her surprise that Sally was blushing and did not seem to know where to turn her eyes. Finally, the second young man moved over to the Wicka buggy, continuing his song.

"Sally, he was singing to you!" exclaimed Annie in a breathy whisper. Sally did not answer. Her face was still rosy pink.

"You're not going to get married soon, are you?" asked Annie fearfully. She did not want to imagine not having Sally there to tell her things.

"No, you silly goose," answered Sally firmly. "It will be a long time before I get married."

But Annie was not so sure about that. Somehow, Sally had seemed pleased and excited when the young man sang to her. If St. Frances of Rome could marry at eleven, then Sally could marry young, too. She had just had her fourteenth birthday. That was a whole lot older than eleven.

Pa came out with the pony of beer.

"I'm sorry it took so long," he apologized to Ma. "Seems as though everyone around was in there, wanting to get waited on."

"Oh, we had a fine entertainment while we were waiting," said Ma with a chuckle. She told Pa all about the young men.

"And one of them has his eye on our Sally," Ma concluded with a laugh.

"You don't say!" exclaimed Pa. He turned around in the buggy to look directly at his oldest daughter. Sally squirmed and blushed again.

"Pa, he was just fooling around," protested Sally.

"I guess he was at that," agreed Pa. "It will be a few years yet before our first girl gets ready to feather her own nest, wouldn't you say so, Anna?"

Ma simply nodded her head. Then she added quietly: "She's such a big help to me I don't know what I would do without her."

Sometimes Annie was jealous when Ma said that. She wanted to be considered a "big help," too, but Ma almost never called her that. Today she was glad to hear Ma's words. That meant Sally was surely going to stay with them for a long time, and not get married.

"It's bad enough wondering if Pa and Ma are going to stay on the farm," thought Annie. "I don't want to think about Sally leaving." So she tried to push out of her mind the picture of the young man singing. For some reason, though, it always came back to her, even in her dreams.

151

Church Picnic

Late in June Ma was reading the newspaper one day after supper.

"There's going to be an eclipse of the sun tomorrow," she said.

"What's that?" asked Annie.

"It's when the moon comes between the earth and the sun and makes it get dark outside."

"Like during the night?"

"Maybe not quite so dark. Do you want to see it? You have to get up early—by six o'clock. The eclipse is supposed to come at ten after six."

"Wake me up. I want to see it," said Annie.

"I do, too," said Sally.

John and Joe groaned. They had to be up by that time no matter what, to start milking the cows with Ma and Pa. They would have liked to stay in bed longer.

"You'd never catch me getting out of bed just for an eclipse," said John.

The next morning Ma woke Sally and Annie at six, but she did not sound too hopeful.

"It's so cloudy this morning. I don't think we'll see much of anything."

Sally and Annie did not get dressed but just wrapped their shawls around their shoulders and went down in their nightgowns. Ma and Pa were standing in the front yard with Joe and John. They were going to wait to start the milking.

The sky was covered with thick gray clouds hanging low. A warm dampness hung in the air. It felt as though it might start raining at any moment.

At ten after six, the sky grew darker and murkier. It looked more like evening than morning. Finally it lightened a little.

"That was a mighty uninteresting show," said Pa. Annie had to agree with him.

But it was the only disappointment of the summer. The rest of the weeks were filled with busy, happy days. There were always hoeing or weeding or haying or chores to be done, but the long, bright days also seemed to have enough time for playing and dreaming.

The corn grew tall and green; the thick oats and buckwheat slowly turned golden. No matter where she walked or looked, Annie felt she was in a green-and-gold bowl, with the blue sky for a cover.

And then there was the church picnic to look forward to, on the last Sunday in August. People would come from miles around, even from Winona, to eat the delicious food, play games, and listen and dance to the music of the Pine Creek band. Last year Ma had not been feeling well so they had stayed only for a short while. This year, Ma said they could stay until it was time to come back for chores and milking in the late afternoon.

"I hope I win the bicycle," said John wishfully.

"Don't get your hopes too high," said Pa. "There's likely to be a thousand people there, all wishing the same thing."

"But you did buy the chances, Pa, didn't you?" asked Annie anxiously. She yearned for the bicycle as much as John and the only way they could win it was if Pa bought chances for it, and for all the other prizes that were being offered.

"I bought a whole book of chances," Pa answered, "and I signed one of our names on every one."

At last the day arrived. Before going off to church, they fed all the animals an extra amount and carried water to the tanks and containers where they drank. Ma picked up her huge basket of food, shut the house up tight, and they were off.

The Mass seemed to take especially long, but at last it was over. Then there was nothing for the children to do but play in the yards and fields while waiting for dinner to be ready. The grown-ups worked hard, preparing the food, setting up long tables in the church basement, and finishing and polishing the wooden dance platform that had been built in the yard at the side of the church.

Annie spotted a group of her classmates racing around in a game of tag.

"I think I'll go play with them," she said.

They chased each other up and around the church,

around the priest's house, behind the school, and even up to the cemetery. When she got tired of tag, Annie jumped rope with Emeline and Helen, two of the girls who would be in second grade with her in September. Finally, the three girls had enough of jumping.

"Let's play crack the whip," suggested Helen. They joined more children and soon had a long, snaking line that moved first one way and then the other, depending on how the leader "cracked the whip."

"I feel as free as a barn swallow," thought Annie as she swooped up and down the field. She did not have to mind her brothers; she did not have to work at anything; she did not have to sit still. Yet, like a barn swallow checking its nest, she would always go and find Ma or Pa every half-hour or so, just to see that they were still there.

"You can sit down and eat in about fifteen minutes," said Ma during one of Annie's flying visits. For once the children got to eat first, with the men and women who were doing the cooking and serving and other work. After that, they were supposed to stay out of the way so their parents could serve all the visitors, who usually started coming after twelve o'clock.

Even though it was only a little after eleven, Annie was so hungry she knew she could eat all the delicious things Ma would pile on her plate. All around her were long, long tables, filled with chattering people who seemed to be talking as much as they were eating.

"I'm not going to say a word," thought Annie. "I'm just going to eat."

At one end of her table sat the men from the band. Their bright blue jackets were full of shiny buttons. Stiff red brushlike tufts stood up from the crowns of their hats, which sat in a line down the middle of the table. The musicians were not eating too much because they had to start playing at noon.

"Run along now," said Ma to Annie and the boys as soon as they had finished eating. "Wait! Here is a nickel for each of you. You may buy ice cream when they open the stand." Ma pressed a nickel into Annie's hand and she gave four nickels to John so he could buy ice cream for himself and Roman and Leo and August.

"Come on, Annie, let's go!" Helen and Emeline were tugging at her.

"What shall we play now?" asked Helen.

"I'm too full to play," said Annie. "Let's sit and wait for the band."

They flung themselves down on the grass at the edge of the platform and waited. The poplar trees cast a wavery shadow over the spot. Helen and Emeline lay there, saying nothing. Annie closed her eyes.

"I can see sparkles and colors on my eyelids," she said softly. Helen and Emeline continued their silence.

Toot! Toot! Wheet! Wheet! Annie jumped up with a start. The men in the band were tuning up their instruments.

"I must have dozed off," she thought. Helen and Emeline were also sitting up with a dazed look in their eyes.

"We fell asleep," they said, rubbing their eyes.

"So did I," laughed Annie. She was glad she was not the only one to have taken a nap, like a baby.

The band started to play and soon the area around the platform was crowded with people. At first, no one stepped up to dance, but when the band swung into the rhythm of a lively polka, one of the men standing at the side cried out: "That's too good to pass up. Come on,

Rosie, we'll be the first to break the ice." He led his wife onto the platform and they began to hop and twirl in time to the music. Soon other couples joined them, and the platform was full of dancers, twisting and skipping and whirling.

"Yoo-hoo-hoo!" yodeled some of the men as they danced.

Now that all the eyes of the spectators were on the platform, Annie turned to Helen.

"Try it with me," she pleaded. She wanted to learn how to dance. Helen locked arms with her and they hopped and skipped over the grass, imitating the older couples. Sometimes their feet got so tangled up with each other, they tumbled down in a heap. Then they would jump up and start over again. Round and round they went until they were out of breath and had to stop. They took turns with Emeline, so she could try dancing, too. Finally, exhausted, they could dance no longer.

"I'm hungry again," cried Annie.

"So am I," answered Emeline. "I have a nickel for ice cream. We can share it."

"I have a nickel, too," said Annie, ashamed she had not offered first.

They walked to the ice-cream stand, which was crowded with children. Inside the stand were several men, turning the handles on wooden ice-cream churns.

"Next batch ready in five minutes," called out the man standing at the counter. "Get your ice-cream cones here. Two big dips in a sweet cone—just five cents, one nickel!"

"What's a cone?" asked Annie.

Before Helen or Emeline could answer, an older boy standing in front of them turned around and snorted.

"You country bumpkins don't even know what an ice-cream cone is? Guess you didn't get to go to the St. Louis World's Fair, like I did," he bragged.

Annie stared at the boy. He was dressed in fancy city clothes. She had never seen him before, so he must have come from Winona; or maybe he came all the way from Chicago or Milwaukee. Some Pine Creek families had relatives who lived in those big cities. Sometimes they came to visit for the summer.

Annie and Helen and Emeline were silent and embarrassed. They didn't answer the boy.

"Ice cream's ready! Who's next?" asked the man at the counter. Two girls put down their nickels and Annie could see the man dip a round spoon into the ice-cream bucket. When he lifted it out, it was filled with creamy, thick ice cream. He plopped it into something that looked like a cookie in the shape of a giant pine cone, only hollow.

"That must be an ice-cream cone," thought Annie. It was the first time she had seen one.

The two girls moved away and the line pressed forward. Soon it was the turn of the city boy.

"Give me *four* dips, in one cone," he ordered, putting two nickels on the counter.

"I don't know as I can get four dips in one cone," said the man. "But I'll try."

He pressed the first spoonful down into the cone. On top of that he put another. Then another and another. The ice cream started to drip down his hand.

"Hurry! Hand it over!" cried the boy. He reached for the cone and began licking the top and sides, trying to stop the dripping.

Then it was Annie's and Emeline's turn. While they

with a name written on it.

"Mrs. Martin Brom wins the lap robe," cried the announcer.

"That's Helen's mother," thought Annie. She was glad she had picked the name of someone she knew. But still, it was not enough to take her mind off Grandfather and Grandmother and the farm.

When she sat down again she saw that Ma had come to join their family group.

"Why such a sour face, Anienka? Aren't you happy Mrs. Brom won that nice prize?" asked Ma.

Before Annie could say a word, Grandmother spoke.

"She just learned that we've sold the farm and are moving soon to Dodge."

"I'll miss them, too, Anienka. But we must look at the bright side," said Ma. "They can take it easy now. And Dodge isn't so very far. We can still see them every week."

Annie hung her head. She knew she should smile at Grandmother, to show her she was glad for her, but she could not bring herself to do it.

The announcer droned on and on, his voice getting higher and higher as he described each prize as better than the one before it. Annie barely listened.

At last came the bicycle, and then she did sit up. So far, no one in their family had won a prize. A boy picked out the chance and handed it to the announcer. The announcer read it, opened his mouth to say something, and then closed it again. He looked over in their direction and smiled.

"Maybe that means I won," thought Annie, and her heart pounded so hard it gave her chest a tight feeling.

"The winner is—" the announcer paused, took a deep

breath, and said: "John Dorawa!"

"I won! I won!" shrieked John, and he started dancing up and down.

"Hold on a minute there," laughed Pa. "My name is John Dorawa, too, you know!" At this, John looked so downcast that Pa gave him a push. "All right, you go up and accept it."

John hopped up to the stage to the sound of clapping all around. His classmates were whistling and stamping their feet. He wheeled the bicycle off to the side where his family was waiting.

"I plain forgot that there were two of us with the same name," Pa was saying. "So I don't rightly know whose chance it was." He turned again to John. "We'll let you consider the bicycle yours, but you have to let your brothers and sisters get their share of riding it. And I want no quarreling over it. Share and share alike. You hear me?"

"Yes, Father," answered John. He was so happy he would have agreed to anything.

Annie stood next to the bicycle. It was so high! She would never be able to ride it alone.

"I'll give you plenty of rides, and hold you on," John assured her. "Don't worry, I wouldn't let you fall."

"Time to go home for chores," said Pa. "I think we've won all the prizes we're going to get for today." They said "Goodbye" to Grandfather and Grandmother.

Amidst the admiring glances of all the families, John wheeled the bicycle over to the buggy.

"I think I'd better ride it home, Pa," he said. "It won't fit very well on the buggy."

"Can you manage it?" asked Pa.

"I've practiced a lot on Uncle Joe's bicycle, in Winona," John assured him.

John followed the buggy all the way home. Sometimes, going uphill, he had to get off and push and then he got far behind. But then he would coast downhill in a whiz, and would always catch up.

"It won't be too long before I learn to ride," thought Annie. "Then I can bicycle all the way to Dodge to visit Grandmother and Grandfather." She pictured herself riding down the hills. Maybe it wasn't going to be so bad after all, having them move away from the farm.

Bumblebee Recess

It was the second week of school. The September weather was still warm and soft. Everywhere, there seemed to be late flowers or clover in bloom and bees buzzing as they tried to gather in the last batches of nectar for their winter supplies.

Annie skipped and hopped, sometimes running ahead of Sally and her friends and sometimes tagging along behind, or bumping into them from the side.

"Stop it!" ordered Sally.

"What?" asked Annie, surprised. She wasn't doing anything.

"You're making me nervous with all that jumping

around," complained Sally. She wanted to walk nicely and talk with the other girls. They had so much to catch up on after the long summer.

Annie felt crushed. She looked at Bibiana and Serafina and Florence. They walked quietly behind Sally and the older girls, listening to everything that was said. Usually, Annie liked to do that, too. You never knew when you would learn something interesting. The older girls often talked about things grown-ups would not discuss—at least, not in front of children.

But today, she didn't feel like walking sedately. She wanted to dance and run and jump, all the way to school.

"I'll walk with the boys, so there!" pouted Annie. She looked back to see how far behind they were. They had stopped next to a field of clover on one side of the road. She walked back toward them.

"I've got one!" John yelled, just as Annie came up to the boys. They didn't even notice her.

"Are you sure it's the right kind?" asked Damazy. "The kind without the stinger?"

"Sure I'm sure," answered John, but he carefully lifted the cover on his dinner pail just a crack, and tried to peer inside. Annie could hear a buzzing sound and soft thuds against the sides of the pail.

"What you got in there?" she asked.

"A bumblebee," answered John.

Now Annie could see that most of the other boys had set their dinner pails in the middle of a patch of clover. The covers were off and they were waiting for a bumblebee to settle inside each one. Roman held tightly to the handle of his pail. He had only started first grade and preferred to watch what the others did, before doing it himself.

167

"I still don't think you're right about the stings," said Alex. "I never heard of bumblebees that don't sting." He and Martin stood to one side, holding on to their dinner pails.

"Don't move!" cried Vic. "There's one in my pail." He crept slowly to the spot where the pails were lined up. The others stood frozen, trying not to make any movements.

"Got you!" shouted Vic as he clamped his pail cover on tight.

Suddenly they heard a faint call in the distance.

"John! Annie! Roman! You'll be late for school."

Guiltily, the boys picked up their pails and hurried to catch up with the girls, but not too close.

"Why do you want those bees in your pails?" asked Annie.

"Because," was all John would answer.

They came to Zabinski's farm, where the road turned sharp right. Dan Zabinski came running out to meet them.

"Have you got them?" he asked.

"I have one and so do Vic and Damazy and Tony," announced John, "but the rest don't. Alex won't go along with us. He thinks we'll get stung."

"Aw, c'mon," coaxed Dan. "Yesterday we all said we'd do it—you, too."

"Do what?" asked Annie.

"Hey, you're not supposed to be listening," protested John. "Go on ahead with the girls." Annie moved ahead a little, but not so far away she couldn't hear.

"It's late. We should be in school," insisted Alex.

"Plenty of time," assured Dan. "I looked at the clock before I came out." Then he lowered his voice so Annie could barely hear.

"You know that clover field of ours right on the line with Jereczek's? It's full of bumblebees' nests in the ground. Bernard is probably out there now. We have time to get at least one in every pail, if we hurry."

Running like a pack of noisy dogs, the boys headed for the field, passing Annie and the other girls.

"Where are they off to in such a hurry?" asked Serafina.

Annie didn't answer. Before long, the girls had caught up again, only now the boys weren't in the road. They were all sitting down or stooping over their pails in the clover field.

"You come along to school, John and Roman," yelled Sally as she passed.

"You, too, Vic and Damazy!" ordered Effie.

Annie slowed down. She wanted to see if the boys caught any more bees. Serafina stayed with her.

"What are they doing?" she asked.

"Something with bumblebees," replied Annie.

"Let's sneak up on them and find out," whispered Serafina.

Annie hesitated. "All right," she said.

They crept along the other side of the line fence. It was overgrown with a tangle of brush and small trees. Soon they could hear the boys talking loudly.

"No, don't take that one," John was saying. "See the stinger? We want one without that. They're usually close to the ground, by the nest."

Through a space in the bushes, Annie saw Alex searching carefully among the clover.

"Is this a good one?" he asked.

"Yah, that's the kind," Damazy nodded. "Close your pail, quick!"

"Remember, we wait for the time just after roll call.

Then start letting them out, one by one." John's voice broke up with a laugh. He started to say something else but the other boys hooted and howled and shrieked so loudly Annie could not hear a thing.

"Come on! Let's run before they see us," urged Serafina. She and Annie sped back to the road and hurried until they caught up with the rest of the girls. When they looked back, they could see the boys back on the road, walking fast so as not to be late.

"Should I tell Sally?" wondered Annie. She didn't like being a tattletale. But what if John and Roman got in trouble? Then Pa would really be mad. She was just deciding to hint at something to Sally, when they heard the first bell ringing at the schoolhouse door.

"Oh, my goodness, we're going to be late!" cried Sally as she started to run. Behind them, the girls could hear the boys speeding up as well. They all reached the front porch of the school just as Sister Pelagia rang the second bell. Laughing and panting, they hurried to their classrooms.

Name by name, Sister Pelagia called the roll and one after another the children answered "Present." They said the morning prayer of offering and then sat down. There was a hush of expectancy. Sister glanced over the entire classroom, puzzled by the sudden quiet.

"She knows something is going to happen," thought Annie, and a tight feeling settled in her middle.

"Grade One, come forward for your reading lesson," said Sister. "Grades Two and Three, copy the arithmetic problems from the board and begin solving them."

"At least," thought Annie, "Roman won't be able to get near his dinner pail." She was not sure if he had a bee in it or not.

The first-graders began to drone out their oral reading of syllables while the older children took out their notebooks and began to copy the numbers on the board. In a few moments the only sound that broke the stillness was Roman's voice as he sounded out syllables.

Bzzzz.

Annie's head flew up. Was that a buzzing noise?

Bzzzz. Bzzzz. Yes it was! One of the bumblebees was out! She could not see it, but she could hear it. Cautiously, she glanced around to see if she could tell who had opened his dinner pail. All heads were bent over their papers.

Bzzzz. Bzzzz. Bzzzz. The noise grew louder, and now the bumblebee flew lazily over the heads of the first-graders, standing in the front. Most of them stopped

171

paying attention to the reading and followed the bee with their eyes, ducking their heads when it came near them.

"Just a moment," said Sister Pelagia. "Grade One, return to your seats." Sister Pelagia took the long window stick and opened the windows wide, from the top. Taking off her apron, she flapped it in the air at the bumblebee.

Someone in the classroom snickered.

"That will be enough," said Sister Pelagia. "The next one to laugh will have to come up and chase the bumblebee out."

Silence fell again on all the children.

"Shoo! Shoo!" Sister Pelagia continued to flap the apron, guiding the bee over to the open windows.

Annie wanted so much to laugh, she had to draw in her breath to stop herself.

At last the bee flew lazily out the window, then in again, then out for good. Sister quickly shut all the windows, except for a crack.

"Grade One, come forward and continue the reading lesson."

The children marched up, carrying their readers. Hardly had they started again when a soft buzzing noise came once more from the back of the room. It grew louder and louder.

Sister glanced up sharply.

"Is that another bumblebee?" she asked.

"Yes, Sister," chorused the children sitting in back.

"Where on earth are they coming from?" she asked, moving toward the rear of the classroom. "Is there a nest of them back here, I wonder? Edmund, did you see where the bumblebee came from?"

"No, Sister," answered Edmund truthfully. He had not seen a thing.

Annie hoped and prayed Sister would not call on her for an answer.

Once again, Sister had the children sit down while she took off her apron and flapped it about until the second bumblebee was out of the window. Then, back to their places in front of the classroom went the first-grade reading class. Five minutes had not gone by before a loud buzzing was heard, coming from the back of the room. This time, Sister Pelagia looked very angry.

The bumblebee was buzzing and circling over Serafina's head.

"Serafina, did you see where the bee came from?" asked Sister.

Serafina blushed and looked down at the floor.

"Serafina, I asked you a question." Sister spoke in her sternest voice. "Where did that bee come from?"

"From one of the boys' dinner pails," blurted out Serafina unhappily. Annie could see she was almost ready to cry.

"Which one of the boys?" asked Sister.

"Oh, no!" thought Annie. "Now Serafina will have to tell." No one wanted to be a tattletale, but when Sister asked like that, you had to tell the truth. There was no getting around it.

"From Vic's," answered Serafina at last.

"So!" Sister paused and took a deep, breathy sigh. "Did you see where the other bumblebees came from?"

Serafina slowly nodded her head. "Yes, Sister," she whispered.

"Did they also come from Victor's dinner pail?"

Serafina shook her head.

"Where did they come from, then?" Sister asked in a cold, tight voice.

The entire classroom was so silent, the buzzing of the

173

third bumblebee sounded like the drone of a sawmill. Everyone waited to hear what Serafina would answer.

"All the boys have them in their dinner pails," said Serafina, and she burst into tears.

Sister looked astonished.

"You mean all the boys in the school?"

Serafina nodded, trying to control her sobs.

"So! So!" said Sister, with a long pause between each word. "Emeline, go and ask Sister Jolanta and Sister Pulcharia to come to the classroom door as soon as possible."

As they waited, the class could hear only the bumblebee and Serafina's noisy sobbing.

"There's no need to cry," said Sister. "Go to the washroom and rinse off your face."

"That's what you think!" said Annie to herself. "If I were Serafina, I'd be crying, too. Now she'll always be called a tattletale."

Emeline came back and slid into her seat. Sister Pelagia went to the hall outside the classroom and the children could hear a murmur of conversation among the three teachers. In a few minutes, Sister returned. She went immediately to pick up the window stick, but did not go to open the windows.

"Is she going to beat the boys with that?" wondered Annie.

"Children, we are going to have recess early today. Girls, you may line up by the door. Boys, I want you to bring your dinner pails up to the front desk. As soon as we are out the door, you are to open them up and let out all the bumblebees. Then you must somehow see to it that they all get outside, through the windows." Sister handed the stick to Edmund.

"Why can't we just—" Dan started to speak but Sister interrupted him.

"Silence! You will do as I say. Since you planned to let them out of your pails for me to chase out through the windows, we shall see how well you like your scheme now that *you* have to get rid of them. I shall stand by the door to see that you're quick about it."

The girls began to file out into the hallway. Annie could see the girls from the other two rooms, also lining up to go out the door. She walked outside and around to the side of the school where their classroom was. Through the windows she could see Vic, Vince, Dan and Edmund, waving their arms wildly.

"I wonder if it's the same in the middle-grade room?" she thought. Swiftly she sped around to the other side of the school, where she could see into the windows of that classroom. There were John and Alex and Damazy and all the other boys, madly chasing after bumblebees with notebooks or rulers in their hands. From the classroom above, she could hear similar sounds.

"Even the seventh- and eighth-grade boys got caught," thought Annie.

The older girls went off to sit quietly on the grass and talk, but the girls from the lower grades ran back and forth from the windows of one classroom to the other. Whenever a bumblebee came flying out, they would give a cheer and start clapping. Once Annie saw John grinning at her through the window.

"Why, they're having as much fun during this recess as we are," she thought. "That's no punishment for them." She wasn't sure whether that made her glad or sorry.

It took the boys a long time to get the bees out—much longer than the usual recess period. At last the bell rang, telling them it was safe to come in again.

Annie lined up with her classmates and they walked in. The boys were sitting in their places—all except Dan. He was standing in front and Sister Pelagia was putting a lump of wet mud on a big, swollen bump, right in the middle of his arm.

"He got stung," Annie said under her breath. "They thought they picked only the bees without stingers, but one of them must have been the stinging kind."

"You see what can happen?" said Sister Pelagia grimly. "Let that be a lesson to you all."

They worked studiously for the rest of the morning and then it was time to eat. Everyone crowded around Dan, wanting to have a look at his bee sting. Only Serafina stayed off to one side.

"You tattletale!" "Squawker!" "Squealer!" some of the boys taunted her. She started crying again and ran off to eat by herself.

Annie felt sorry for her. "What if Sister had asked me first?" she wondered. "Would I have told the truth? Then *I* would be the tattletale." Quietly, she slipped off to the side of the school where Serafina had disappeared. She found her sitting on the side steps.

"I'll eat dinner with you and then play," offered Annie.

"I don't want to eat or play with nobody!" cried Serafina. She turned her face away.

"Okay for you!" muttered Annie as she walked off. "No need to get mad at me."

But the more she thought about it, the more she realized that she would probably feel just like Serafina, if she had told on the boys.

"Grown-ups just don't know how hard it is to tell the truth sometimes," thought Annie.

Chop Off the Chicken's Head

"You're to mind Joe and do what he tells you, you hear, Annie?"

"Yes, Pa."

"And you, Joe and John—no fooling around," warned Pa.

"No, Pa," said the two boys in unison.

"Remember to do the chickens for me, Joe, so that we have something for dinner tomorrow." Ma's voice was gentler than Pa's.

Finally the instructions were complete and the buggy departed. Pa and Ma were going to Winona with Grandfather, to take care of some legal business. Sally would stay with Grandmother in Dodge and help her get settled in the new place. The younger boys would stay there, too.

"I'm a little lonesome," Grandmother had said at church last Sunday. "I need some company."

Annie was glad to be staying home for once. It would give her a chance to practice riding the bicycle. She wanted to start as soon as the buggy was gone, but Joe put a stop to that.

"No bicycle riding until the barn is cleaned," he said as he went off in that direction. John followed him reluctantly.

Annie stared at the bicycle propped up against the wire fence in front of their house. Joe hadn't said she couldn't sit on it. He only said "no riding." She climbed to the high seat and stretched her legs on either side of the top bar. Her feet just reached the pedals. One handlebar leaned against the fence and Annie tried to pry it loose and set it straight. The bicycle rolled about a foot forward and she wobbled on the seat until the handlebar caught on a post.

"I didn't fall off!" she cried. Maybe if she could get the handlebars all the way away from the post and wires of the fence, she could move the bicycle back and forth, holding on to the fence with one hand.

"You get away from that bicycle," yelled Joe from the barn door. "Else you won't get to ride it at all later on. You could come and give us a hand, you know."

Guiltily, Annie climbed off the bicycle and went to the barn. If there was one job she disliked, it was helping with the barn cleaning. All the smelly manure had to be scraped out of the gutters with shovels and the wet bedding straw forked out of the stalls and put into the manure spreader. As soon as the spreader was full, Joe hitched up a team of horses and drove it out to empty over the bare fields. Annie didn't understand how it worked, but somehow the manure made the crops grow better the next year.

"You could throw down the fresh straw," suggested Joe.

"Okay," agreed Annie. That wasn't nearly as bad as scraping the manure. She climbed to the top of the straw pile that stood next to the sliding side door. After tossing down quite a few armfuls of dry, prickly straw, she slid down and began to carry the straw into the barn stalls that were already clean.

She and the boys worked for more than two hours and didn't leave the barn until they had spread fresh, clean straw all over the floor.

"Now can we ride the bicycle?" asked Annie.

"First gather the eggs and feed the chickens," said Joe. "I don't think Sally had time to do it. Then you can ride the bicycle until dinnertime."

Annie and John hurried to the chicken coop. As fast as they could they spread the mash and chopped corn into the troughs, filled the drinking pans with water, and gathered in all the eggs. They carried them to the cellar where Ma kept the egg crates.

"Now, to the bicycle!" gloated John. "I'll take it for a ride to warm it up." Annie wanted to argue with him, but then she remembered Pa's warning.

John climbed on the bicycle, rode around the yard a few times, and then cycled down the road leading to the valley road. It curved gently and was just right for getting up a good speed. Annie watched until he disappeared from sight.

179

It was a long time before he appeared again, standing up on the pedals and pumping as hard as he could. He always tried to make it up the hill without getting off the bicycle, but he never could. He always had to get off and push the bicycle up the last stretch.

"It's my turn," shouted Annie as soon as he got to the top.

"Give a fellow a chance to catch his breath," panted John.

Annie waited impatiently for a few minutes and then swung herself up on the bicycle seat. Gripping the handlebars tightly, she put her feet on the pedals and pressed down. John hung on to the seat and guided her along.

For at least a hundred times, or so it seemed to Annie, he started her off and then tried to let go. Each time the bicycle wobbled and turned to the side so he had to catch it again. A couple of times he didn't catch it in time and she fell to the ground, scraping her knee.

"Balance yourself and steer at the same time," yelled John. He was getting disgusted.

"I'm trying to," Annie shouted back at him.

He made her stop for a while and then Joe wanted a turn.

"Okay, we'll let you try it a few times more," said Joe when he returned from his ride. "But then it will be time to go in for dinner."

This time *he* held on to the bicycle as Annie steered it up and down the front yard. Each time she could go a little longer before he had to catch her again. At last, he took her up to the farthest part of the yard and started her off in the direction of the house. The yard slanted down a little. Without any warning he let her go. Annie balanced and didn't topple over.

"I'm riding," she thought gleefully. "But now how do I stop?" She steered straight for the fence.

"Put on the brake!" shouted Joe.

Annie tried to remember how the brake worked. Just in time she reversed the pedals and stopped, clutching the fence with one hand.

"Pretty good," said Joe. "A little more practice and you'll do fine. Now it's time to go in for dinner."

"I'm going to practice all afternoon," said Annie.

"Not until we get those chickens butchered and plucked," said Joe.

They hurried through dinner. Ma had left plenty of food to warm up, so it did not take them long to get it on the table. Afterward, Annie washed and dried the dishes.

Joe put the kettle over the warmest part of the fire, so it would boil. Then he took out a large enamel pan and handed it to John.

"Take this out to the chopping block. I'll go get the chickens," he said as he left the house.

John picked up the pan and started walking to the back of the woodpile, where Pa kept the ax and a small hatchet wedged into cracks in the round, fat stump of wood he used for a chopping surface. Annie followed him.

Next to the chopping block was a whetstone. John held the hatchet against the stone, grinding its edge until it was shiny and sharp. Annie moved in closer to watch him.

"You're not supposed to be here," said John. That was true. If Pa ever caught Annie or the younger boys near the chopping block, he gave them a spanking.

"You wait until you're old enough for me to teach you how to handle it," he always said. "Until then, stay away from there."

But Annie thought she was now old enough to be by

the chopping block. "After all," she thought, "I can almost ride the bicycle." She decided to stay with John.

He was practicing with the hatchet, testing to see if it was sharp enough. Chop! He whacked it into a piece of wood. Then he ground it more on the whetstone.

Annie had an idea. She held a stick of wood on the block.

"Try it now," she said. John brought the hatchet down, but as soon as he did, Annie pulled the stick away. The hatchet stuck fast in the chopping block.

"Ha! Ha! I fooled you!"

John pulled out the hatchet, wrenched the stick of wood away from Annie and threw it back on the woodpile. He was mad.

Then a spiteful feeling spread through Annie. Ever afterward, she would wonder where that meanness came from, but there it was. It made her do a dreadful thing!

She put her pointing finger on the chopping block and called out to John, in a taunting voice.

"Bet you can't chop off this chicken's head!"

John looked at her. Then he lifted the hatchet over her finger and pretended to bring it down. Quick as a wink, Annie slid her finger away, even though John didn't bring the hatchet down all the way.

"Chop off the chicken's head!" taunted Annie again. Slyly, she slid her finger over the chopping block.

Once more John brought down his hatchet part way, and Annie snapped her finger away.

"Ha! Ha! You'll never catch this chicken's head," Annie bragged. John was furious but he didn't say a word. That made Annie feel even meaner. She wanted to get his goat.

"Chop off the chicken's head! Chop off the chicken's head!" she chanted, snaking her finger on and off the chopping block.

John raised his hatchet. He was going to give her a good scare.

Chop! He brought it down suddenly, with all his might, at the precise moment that Annie slid her finger on the block. The hatchet sliced right through the tip of her finger and the blood spurted out.

Both John and Annie were so horrified, they didn't move for a few moments. The blood continued to gush out of the tip of her finger.

Luckily, Joe came up just then, carrying three squawking chickens by their legs.

"Jesus, Mary and Joseph," he prayed. Dropping the chickens he ran into the house, calling back over his shoulder: "Stay there. Don't move." He came hurrying out with a big dishtowel. Round and round Annie's finger he wound it, but as fast as he worked, the blood worked faster, oozing through the thick cotton cloth.

"Run in and get another towel," he ordered. In seconds, John was back with an armful of dishtowels that he had grabbed from the kitchen drawer.

Joe twisted one of the towels around Annie's upper arm, so tight she could feel it turning numb. Still, she did not cry out or even whimper.

"I'll have to take her to Galesville," said Joe. That was where the closest doctor lived. "Watch her while I hitch up." It took him about ten minutes, but still Annie did not say a word, or even move. She just sat there by the chopping block.

Then Joe lifted her up to the buggy seat. It was the small, old one-seat buggy that they hardly ever used.

"Hold your arm up," he instructed her. "Like this."

They rode all the way to Galesville without talking. The rough stones in some parts of the road gave Annie a twinge of pain in her arm, but she hardly noticed it. She sat and stared straight ahead, clinging to the buggy seat with her left hand as Joe clattered along as fast as he could urge the horses to go.

It took them about forty minutes to get there. Joe pulled the horses to a halt in front of the clinic and lifted Annie down.

"Can you walk?" he asked. Annie nodded her head.

They entered the clinic and Annie saw the eyes of everyone there swerve to the blood-soaked towel around her finger.

"There's been an accident," said Joe to the nurse at the desk. She took one look at Annie's hand and hurried them into the doctor's office. The doctor was washing his hands, and he did not waste any time on words. He

unwound the bloody towel and carefully examined Annie's finger.

Annie closed her eyes. Something pinched dreadfully
and then she fluttered her eyelids open long enough to
see the doctor sewing up the tip of her finger.

"There! It'll soon be as good as new, only a little shorter
than before," announced the doctor. Annie felt him
spread a salve over the entire finger and then bandage it.
Then she opened her eyes.

"She's a brave little girl," said the doctor to Joe. "Not a
peep out of her." Joe said nothing.

Annie didn't feel brave. She felt ashamed and sorry.
She wanted to cry, but the tears wouldn't come. The
doctor made her swallow some medicine dissolved in
water.

"You'd better take it nice and slow going home,"
whispered the doctor to Joe. "She's still suffering from
shock."

Joe lifted Annie into the buggy. She felt awkward, not
being able to climb in by herself. He drove the horses
homeward, keeping them at a slow walk. Annie's finger
throbbed.

"Pa and Ma are probably home already," said Joe as he
turned in at the valley road.

Annie did not answer him. She did not want to think of
the moment when she had to face Ma and Pa, so she
forced it to go away back into a corner of her mind.

The horses picked up speed. They were anxious to get
home, even though Annie was not. Up the hill and into
the front yard they trotted. There, lined up by the fence
in front of the house, were Pa, Ma, Sally, John and the
little boys, all staring at her.

"Whoa!" said Joe, and as soon as the buggy stopped Pa

came forward and lifted Annie out. She ran to Ma, and then the flood of tears broke loose.

"Oh, Ma! Oh, Ma!" was all she could say as sob after sob shuddered through her. Ma held her close and stroked her back.

"It's going to be all right. It's going to be all right," she repeated, over and over.

Annie was crying so hard and loud, she didn't see Pa talking to the older boys. She didn't see him go to the kitchen to get his razor strap. And she didn't see him take Joe and John behind the woodpile, with the razor strap in hand.

But she did notice the strap after Pa came around the woodpile again.

"No, Pa, don't give them a strapping," screamed Annie. "It was all my fault."

"I've already done it," said Pa seriously. "Joe did the right thing, taking you to Galesville; but he and John were wrong to let you go by the chopping block. I don't like using the strap any more than they like feeling it, but I don't know any other way to teach them their duties." He looked sad and sorry.

"Come, Annie, I want you to lie down for a little before supper," said Ma. "You'll work yourself into a fever." She guided Annie into the downstairs bedroom.

Annie lay there, thinking and thinking. It didn't seem fair that Pa strapped the boys, when she had been the one to start it all.

"If only I hadn't put my finger on that chopping block!" thought Annie.

"But you did!" said the Voice inside her.

"I was only teasing," Annie defended herself.

"You were being mean," insisted the Voice. "When

you're bad, you not only hurt yourself, you hurt others, too."

The realization of what that meant passed all over her body, like the prickles of the patch of nettles she had once fallen in. She tossed and turned on the bed, as though trying to get rid of an itchy feeling. But it wouldn't go away.

"Time for supper," Sally called softly from the bedroom door. Slowly, Annie got up and went to the kitchen. Joe and John were washing up in the basin on the bench by the door. She walked over to them.

"You're not mad at me, are you?" she whispered. "I told Pa it was my fault."

"Naw," said Joe, wiping his face on the roller towel. "I should have been watching you, like Pa said."

"Besides," said John, "a strapping ain't nothing compared to losing your fingertip."

"They are the best brothers in the whole world," thought Annie gratefully. She forgot all about the times they quarreled and she forgot about the meanness they sometimes felt toward each other.

"Come to the table," called Ma.

They sat down and recited the prayer before meals. Everyone began to eat.

Annie stared at her right hand with the heavy bandage on the pointing finger. She touched her fork lightly, but didn't pick it up. Then she burst into tears again.

"Now what are you crying about?" asked Pa.

"I can't use my right hand," wailed Annie. "Now I won't be able to eat or do anything to be a 'big help' to Ma, when Sally gets married. Then you'll sell the farm and we'll move to town and I don't want to!" She sobbed and sobbed as her family stared at her.

Pa reached over and shook her shoulder hard.

"Now stop that, you hear? Joe told me the doctor said your finger will be fine in a week or two. You'll be able to use it same as ever, and help Ma just like Sally does."

"And I'm *not* getting married soon," interrupted Sally.

"As for selling the farm and moving to town," continued Pa, "that's not likely to happen until we're as old as Grandfather and Grandmother. Here on the farm we always have food and know where our next meal is coming from. And there's room to let a fellow breathe; it's not closed in, like in town. So just forget all that nonsense and eat your supper."

"Here," said Ma, handing Annie the fork. "Be our clever little girl, like you usually are; try holding it in your other fingers."

Annie stretched her pointing finger out of the way and grasped the fork between her thumb and the other fingers. It was awkward, but she could hold it pretty well. She forked some potatoes into her mouth.

"You see," said Ma. "It works!"

Annie smiled at everyone around the table. Her brothers grinned back at her. She ate and ate, now that she realized how hungry she was. The finger got in her way now and then, and it still throbbed. The pain was starting to come back now that the numbness was almost gone.

"But I'm not going to cry anymore," said Annie to herself. "I'm going to be a clever girl, like Ma wants me to be." She wondered if she would be able to hold a pencil, as she was holding her fork. Back in the corner of her mind sprang up a picture of herself, showing her finger to her classmates.

"It's not something to brag about or show off," said the Voice inside her.

"I know," thought Annie. She was truly sorry she had been so naughty, and truly sorry that she had lost her fingertip. It was gone, and there was nothing she could do about it.

"I won't brag about it," said Annie to herself, "but I'll show it to them if they want to see it."

"Come, Annie," said Ma as soon as they finished eating. "You look feverish. I want you to go to bed right away." Ma crushed an aspirin and dissolved it in water. Annie swallowed the bitter liquid and lay back on her pillow. She felt relief flow through her like hot soup on a cold day.

"It wasn't worth losing my fingertip," she thought sleepily, "but I'm so glad I know for sure we're not leaving the farm. Pa won't change his mind now."

Through the drowsy haze in her mind she pictured their house, their barns, their sheds and pens: there were Pa and Ma and Sally and her brothers, taking care of the animals and doing their chores. She saw herself playing with two frisky lambs. They were running and jumping so high they almost seemed to be flying. Suddenly, one of the lambs flew up into the sky and turned into a fluffy cloud. Annie felt herself being pulled along by the cloud and then the picture faded. She was fast asleep.

Pronunciation Guide

A000120005961